DEER LIFE

DEER LIFE

A FAIRY TALE

RON SEXSMITH

DUNDURN
TORONTO

Cover image: istock.com/modera76
Interior illustrations: Ron Sexsmith
Printer: Webcom

Library and Archives Canada Cataloguing in Publication

Sexsmith, Ron, 1964-, author
    Deer life / Ron Sexsmith.

Issued in print and electronic formats.
ISBN 978-1-4597-3877-5 (softcover).--ISBN 978-1-4597-3878-2 (PDF).--
ISBN 978-1-4597-3879-9 (EPUB)

I. Title.

PS8637.E938D44 2017   C813'.6   C2016-907755-1
                                             C2016-907756-X

1 2 3 4 5   21 20 19 18 17

    Conseil des Arts du Canada   **Canada Council for the Arts**    ONTARIO ARTS COUNCIL CONSEIL DES ARTS DE L'ONTARIO an Ontario government agency un organisme du gouvernement de l'Ontario

We acknowledge the support of the **Canada Council for the Arts**, which last year invested $153 million to bring the arts to Canadians throughout the country, and the **Ontario Arts Council** for our publishing program. We also acknowledge the financial support of the **Government of Ontario**, through the **Ontario Book Publishing Tax Credit** and the **Ontario Media Development Corporation**, and the **Government of Canada.**

Nous remercions **le Conseil des arts du Canada** de son soutien. L'an dernier, le Conseil a investi 153 millions de dollars pour mettre de l'art dans la vie des Canadiennes et des Canadiens de tout le pays.

Care has been taken to trace the ownership of copyright material used in this book. The author and the publisher welcome any information enabling them to rectify any references or credits in subsequent editions.

— *J. Kirk Howard, President*

The publisher is not responsible for websites or their content unless they are owned by the publisher.

Printed and bound in Canada.

VISIT US AT

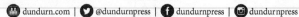 dundurn.com | @dundurnpress | dundurnpress | dundurnpress

Dundurn
3 Church Street, Suite 500
Toronto, Ontario, Canada
M5E 1M2

To Colleen for encouraging me to write this book and for believing that I could actually write one.... To my adult children, Christopher and Evelyne, as well, who I'll forever miss reading bedtime stories to.

I would also like to dedicate this book to the many writers who've inspired me with their stories, their humour, and their wisdom (Charles Dickens, Mark Twain, Roald Dahl, The Brothers Grimm, Hans Christian Andersen, L. Frank Baum, and Ray Bradbury, to name a few).

CONTENTS

PREFACE   9

PROLOGUE   11

A HISTORY OF HINTHOVEN,   17
    HINTERLUNDS, AND HEDLIGHTS

HINTERLUND HOME   21

JACQUES TOURTIÈRE   25

HEDLIGHT GOES A-HUNTING   28

MEMORIES OF CRAD GRIMSBY   31

IN THE CLEARING   38

FIST AND FIRKIN   43

DEER FRIEND   47

OF MAGGIE AND CRAD AND GRIFF AND GRUFF   52

BEAUTIFUL MORNING   57

OUT OF THE WOODS   62

CRAD'S BIG DAY OUT   67

LUCKY AND CLAIRA   71

HEDLIGHT HOME   77

FROM BAD TO WORSE   83

AUGUSTAFEST   87

THE GATHERING GLOOM   94

AND NOT A MOMENT TO SPARE   101

ENOUGH AS IT IS (IN SIX PARTS)   109

CHANGES   118

EPILOGUE   126

PREFACE

ello and welcome to my book.

As a songwriter, I'd gotten used to waking up with a melodic or lyrical idea in my head, but this time 'round it was different. I could tell right away that this was not a song, but in fact the arc of a story. The idea, which first presented itself to me in a morning dream, had me at a loss in terms of what to do with it.

My first thought was that it could be a screenplay for an animated movie, and I spent the next year or so telling actor friends and getting their take on it. But not knowing the first thing about how to make a movie, I began to think of it as a concept for a children's storybook with illustrations.

Around this time, I got an unexpected email from a prominent publishing house that had heard through the rumour mill that I had a book idea and was interested in hearing all about it. (I realize this is not how it usually works for novelists, but that's what happened.) Anyway, some weeks later I was sitting in their boardroom and relaying the very basic gist of the story across a long table with not a single word of it written down. Well, after hearing me out, they could see it as being more of a novel or novella and encouraged me to go off and write it, AND if possible to have my first draft in by the end of August 2015. (It was March at the time.)

Now, in hindsight, they may have just wanted me to go away. Maybe they didn't think I would actually do it? I'll never know for sure.... Nevertheless, I got right to work on it, writing every day while out touring my latest record, until lo and behold … I delivered my first draft and right on time!

For reasons that are unimportant now, this particular publishing house decided not to go for it, setting into motion a mercifully brief period of rejection and disappointment as I shopped it around.

I was beginning to feel like the laughingstock of the Toronto literary world until it fell into the hands of an editor at Dundurn who seemed not only to like the book, but also to get what I was trying to do.

So as you can imagine, it's with equal parts pride and amazement that I sit here today with this, my first ever work of fiction. I had so many questions along the way about structure and punctuation, pacing, etc., but I kept at it and was surprised to see how so many unforeseen characters and subplots would emerge from what was originally a skeletal arc. And how happy coincidences would occur later in the book that lined up with things I had written in earlier chapters. It was just so different from songwriting in so many ways.

I could see the town and the characters and became attached to them to the point where I was quite sad to see some of them go.

In closing, I'd just like to thank you all in advance for your perusal of it. A fairy tale often requires us to suspend our disbelief for a while in order to come along for the ride.

So with that in mind, I invite you now into this fictional world of magic and loss, friendship and heroism, among other things that are very much rooted in the world we've all come to know.

With love,
Ronald Eldon Sexsmith

PROLOGUE

Leaves in the whirlwind, scarecrow's clappin'
All good children ought to be nappin'.
The cows in the tree, the bird's on the ground
For your dream's just a nightmare upside down.

These were the only lines she could recall of a schoolyard song overheard in passing. Its melody, though, kept them both in good company as it floated on the breeze to the rhythm of their footsteps on gravel.

They'd only been walking a few hours when they saw the light of an inn just up ahead. Their shadows were practically there. Eleanoir and her dog, Jupiter, had found the last town to be a tad unfriendly, even more so than the town before and the town before that — although at first glance, it would be hard to imagine how anyone could take a dislike to either one of them. Eleanoir, for example, was strangely beautiful. (Well, in a frozen lake sort of way, I suppose.) And in keeping with this metaphor, there was never any way of knowing the cold thoughts that swam beneath the surface of her eyes, but then she liked it that way.

As for Jupiter? He was a hybrid, to say the least. Part wolf, part husky, with eyes like frosted windows through which a vague sense of helplessness and other humanlike emotions struggled to see out of. Though at a glance he appeared as loyal as the day or his tail were long. And as far as anyone could tell, this coldly attractive woman was quite possibly his best and only friend. For when you're a dog, one friend is oft times all you get....

Upon reaching the entrance to the inn, a rustic sign that was at first impossible to read came into focus at last. THE WILLOW TREE, it hailed proudly, albeit faintly. The faded etching of a tree, in fact, could still be made out behind the green letters (though whoever the artist was had apparently never seen a willow tree before).

"Well, Jupiter, I hope this place is to your liking," said Eleanoir as the moon rested on her shoulder. Naturally, Jupiter's tail wagged in canine approval.

Once inside, there hung the unmistakable odour of armpits and shame. A few patrons were scattered about the room in various stages of drunkenness while an impressive fire roared in the corner. Not a soul looked up, however, except for the innkeeper, who went by the unfortunate name of Crad Grimsby (a rather beery-looking man, stout but with kind enough features) who came floating over immediately to greet our weary travellers. Even crouching down (with great difficulty) to give Jupiter a pat on the head, creating a flurry of dog whimpering that sounded almost remorseful, or so he thought. "You're a fine boy, aren't ya! Yes, you are!" Crad spoke before struggling (with even greater difficulty) to get back on his feet.

"S'pose you'll be needing a room tonight, ma'am?" he asked once at eye level with Eleanoir. T'was then he noticed the strange purple tint to her eyes, which made all the colour run from his face. He'd seen these sort of eyes before as a child back in Hixenbaugh. Eleanoir had seen his expression before, too.

It was not lost on her. "Mr. Grimsby?" she slyly inquired. "Is there something wrong? You look pale."

"No, ma'am," replied the innkeeper while attempting to collect himself, with decidedly mixed results. "Mistook you for somebody else is all," he said, smiling back nervously. "A sad symptom of age, I'm afraid."

"Really? Well, that's odd," said Eleanoir. "Although I've been told I do look an awful lot like my mother. You know, once upon a time. Maybe you've seen her somewhere before? In Hixenbaugh, perhaps?" she continued as two fingers tiptoed on the edge of her chin. "That is where you're from, is it not?"

At this curious line of questioning, Grimsby's smile faded to make way for a new look of discomfort, which had spread across his pie-shaped countenance like strawberry jam.

"Well, no matter," said Eleanoir with a dismissive laugh. "A room would be lovely. And if possible, could you bring us two bowls of ..." — and glanced skeptically toward the kitchen — "... whatever's in that pot over there, and some wine if you have any?"

"Yes, of course," replied the innkeeper with a newly ruffled energy that darkened his otherwise light demeanour. "Coming right up!" But turning to fetch these items, he stopped short, as if forgetting something of great import, and turned once more to face her.

"I'm sorry, where are my manners? Would you and your furry friend here care to take a seat by the fireside?" came his half-hearted invitation with arms outstretched, as though he'd conjured up the fire with sorcery.

Eleanoir simply shrugged as Jupiter sniffed a curious crumb on the floor. "I guess it has gotten quite chilly out there, hasn't it?" she added.

"Yes, ma'am, winter's heading straight for us, I suspect," Grimsby prattled on while scrunching up his naturally scrunched-up face before scurrying back toward the kitchen. And so, in taking the innkeeper's advice, Eleanoir and Jupiter moved over to the fire, where a drunkard now lay passed out, and in doing so, was taking up two whole seats! Jupiter growled at the unsavoury man, though if for reason of appearance, smell, or both remains a dog's mystery to this very day. But no sooner had I finished writing the above sentence when Grimsby came rushing back as promised with wine and two bowls of something resembling fish soup. But after delicately setting the tray down on a low table near the hearth, he set about indelicately kicking the poor man back to life. "Wake up, Tom, I've warned you! It's not a flophouse we're running here! If you can't stay vertical, then go and be horizontal someplace else."

All of this he barked (and rather unconvincingly, I might add) while glancing toward Eleanoir at intervals, in the hopes of impressing her with these very dubious "take-charge abilities." Even so, at the conclusion of this crude display, our man Tom rose and then mumbled a slurred apology to everyone he'd ever wronged, before staggering off to the other side of the room (where he proceeded to pass out over there!). Soon Eleanoir and dog were warming their bones and enjoying the cozy atmosphere (and dare I say charm?) of The Willow Tree. Even the soup wasn't half bad. "So, where ya heading to, ma'am? If you don't mind me asking, of course," inquired Grimsby from a safe distance behind the bar.

Eleanoir smiled a slightly forced smile and replied, "We're not exactly sure, are we, Jupiter?" For he was just now gazing up at his master with that same pitiful panting face of oblivion shared by dogs everywhere. "How far to the next town?" she then asked, though purely for politeness's sake (she already knew the answer).

"Hmmm, now let me think," said Grimsby. His thoughts indeed went rummaging around his brain before arriving at the word *Hinthoven* after much eyebrow activity. (Though it wasn't in any need of such consideration either, for he'd lived in these parts all his life.) "If I'm not mistaken," he feigned in earnest, "it's just on the other side of these woods. With an early start, you can make it by suppertime," before adding with a sort of ominous emphasis, "I would not recommend going through there at night!"

After which his dark eyes could be seen rolling off in the direction of the forest as he shook his finger to further impress on Eleanoir the gravity of whatever he was implying. "Well, it's awfully kind of you to be so ... concerned," she said, now mindlessly patting Jupiter's head and staring deep into the fire. "We wouldn't dream of it."

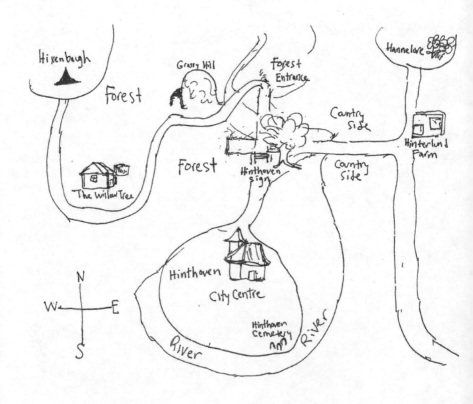

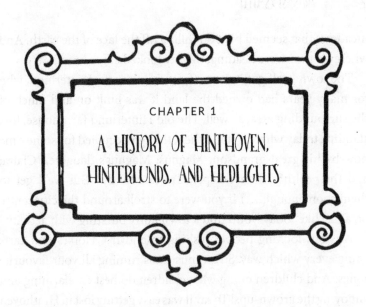

CHAPTER 1

A HISTORY OF HINTHOVEN, HINTERLUNDS, AND HEDLIGHTS

he town of Hinthoven was nothing much to write home about. In fact, no one could even vaguely recall a letter, postcard, or package ever being sent to or from there at any point in time. For this reason and possibly a few others, it has been largely omitted from the pages of history. That is until now. And it is no secret that for many people living in nearby townships, Hinthoven had long been considered the punchline of numerous and humourless jokes. All manner of good-natured ribbing (as well as many not so good-natured things) had been said over the years in taverns and 'round dinner tables, such as "Hinthoven, the city that can't take a hint" or "Squinthoven" (which apparently just sounded funny), and all said by folks who'd never even set foot there!

For the good citizens of Hinthoven, however, it was simply put: "A nice place to call home." People were kind, the air was clean. The water was pure and life in general was … liveable. To look at it on a map, it would appear the whole town was caught in a perpetual headlock between a peaceful river to the east and a menacing forest to the west. Just outside the city centre and to the north a bit lay prime farmland, acres of orchards, vineyards, and plush, rolling meadows that seemed bent on rolling off the face of the earth. And wherever they were heading, the sky looked eager to follow.

The town itself got its name from one Marcus Hinterlund, who for many years had owned the land it was built on and much of the surrounding area, as well. The old Hinterlund farmhouse, too, standing today where it stood then, though occupied for some time now by his great-grandson, Magnus; Magnus's daughter, Claira; and their faithful housekeeper, Tressa Mundy. (But we'll get to them soon enough....) If you were to stroll around the city centre on a day like today, you'd find a town fairly bursting with activity.

Anxious-looking people rushing to and fro. Horses and carts going every which way. Street musicians ruining all your favourite songs. And children doing what children do best ... alarming and annoying the grown-ups! To say it was easy getting lost in Hinthoven would be a huge understatement. Even those who'd spent their entire lives there could find themselves frequently disoriented, as if in a maze. For every street seemed to spiral into another, jut out unexpectedly, or end abruptly, so one was never sure if they were even on the same street they had started out on. You might think the city's forefathers had been inspired by the great mysteries of the universe when designing their street plans. And clearly it had not occurred to any of them that more than one horse and cart might wish to pass down the same street at the same time. For each was ludicrously narrow and filled with pedestrians at all hours.

In fact, it was on one such crowded, narrow street where lived Deryn Hedlight and his mother, Maggie, in an abode so humble that it looked positively mortified to even be mentioned in this book! Today being the anniversary of Pearson Hedlight's death (loving husband to Maggie, stern but patient father to Deryn), we find both in a reflective mood after their sombre gravesite visit. "What do you suppose Dad's doing right now?" asked Deryn innocently enough.

"Well, if I know your father," said Maggie, "and I do! I'd say he's enjoying his pipe right about now. Assuming they let you smoke up there." After which she took a moment to ponder this ancient mystery before vigorously stirring a pot on an old wood stove.

"You know, I never told you," said Deryn after a moment's reflection, "but Dad caught me smoking his pipe one time and —"

"Oh, I know," interrupted Maggie. "Your father and I never had any secrets between us — he told me all about it! Why, I can remember him saying like it was yesterday: 'A man must earn the right to smoke his pipe. At the end of a day's work or after a hunt, when you've brought food home for the table.' And he was right!" she exclaimed while pointing her wooden spoon seemingly t'ward heaven. Deryn looked wistfully at the spoon, then at the rifle hanging over the fireplace. "He was proud of his boy, though," Maggie went on, sensing a shade of doubt in her son's melancholy face. "And don't think for a moment he wasn't!"

"Oh, I know, Ma, I just wish I ..." Deryn's voice trailed off. For his attention was drawn to an imposing shadow now moving across the curtain. The shadow belonged to one Jacques Tourtière, noted hunter and local bully, who at that very moment was pulling a cart of fresh kill from his latest hunt. Tourtière supplied meat for the local butchers and made a pretty penny, too, when he wasn't boozing or beating people up. To say he was well liked in Hinthoven would be a stretch, but if it mattered to him in the slightest, he never let it show. "Better to be feared than loved," he'd often say. To no one in particular. Deryn himself could recall quite a few unpleasant run-ins between his father and Tourtière over the years, so the mere mention of his name could conjure up a whole multitude of emotions. None of which were helpful in any way.

"Ma?" Deryn said after returning to the present.

"Yes, dear?" she replied with eyes peeking over the pot.

"Well, I was thinking that p'raps I'd go hunting tomorrow." This he said with a hopeful yet altogether heartbreaking air. And though looking in the direction of his mother, his eyes were fixed upon a world somewhere beyond her and out past this once cheerful home. "Maybe it's time," he continued, "that I started acting like …" Here he paused to rise heroically from his low seat in the corner. "The man of the house, the man Dad always wanted me to be," he said and finished off with an expression verging on bravery. (Though verging from a good distance, truth be told!) But still pondering the great mystery of pipe smoking in Heaven, Maggie responded as anyone snapping out of a daydream would. "Sorry, dear, were you saying something?"

CHAPTER 2

HINTERLUND HOME

Young Claira Hinterlund was said to be the spitting image of her mother, Camilla. She had no way of knowing this, however, since cameras had not yet been invented. Mostly, though, it was due to the fact that her mother had died not long before her first birthday. In those sad weeks and months following this tragedy, it became apparent to all those concerned that her love was the one light strong enough to reach down into her father's broken heart and shoo away the darkness. And providing a formidable light of her own during this difficult time came their faithful housekeeper, Tressa Mundy. She had been brought in to help around the house when Claira was born and went on to become a source of great comfort as Camilla succumbed to her illness that last sad summer.

Tressa could best be described as kindness in human form. She was naturally pretty, though plain, for her beauty was of the kind that rose from within and shone outward through her eyes. For nearly sixteen years now she'd served as both friend and mother figure to Claira while being an enormous help to Magnus in all aspects of domesticity short of being his wife. Time, it seemed, had truly healed all wounds, while in the process somehow managing to extract the sadness from yesteryear, making it almost seem a pleasant memory. Well, almost....

On this golden autumn day there was much activity as the Hinterlunds prepared for their weekly jaunt into town to buy groceries and other household necessities. Claira very much looked forward to this day, for it often meant stopping by the bakery on their way home to pick up fresh pastries and biscuits. It also meant a change of scene from life in the country, which, as charming as it may very well be, could get a bit dreary at times, let's not kid ourselves. Even Magnus looked forward to it in his own way. He loved getting the horse and wagon ready and didn't much seem to mind donning his less comfortable "city clothes" for the day. As for Tressa, well, she just loved to sit up front with him, for he always looked so handsome, and although he wasn't much of a talker, he was certainly a most excellent listener!

It had rained hard the night before, and so on the road that morning everything seemed new and quite literally dripping with promise. And Tressa, who was in an especially chatty mood, practically overflowed with details of a strange dream involving a hat full of ravens and an enormous tree. Not that anybody minded, for her voice was in no way an unpleasant thing to hear.

Well, it was in the midst of these very dream details when Magnus, who, as always, was half listening (and nodding his head even when he wasn't), noticed a small figure approaching near the Hinthoven sign at the outskirts of town. Why, if it wasn't our very own Deryn Hedlight, rifle in hand and pulling a makeshift cart behind him! "Good morning!" he exclaimed while cheerfully hoisting his gun into the air.

"Good morning to you," replied Magnus with a tight-lipped grin. "You're Pearson Hedlight's boy, aren't you? Deryn, is it?"

"Yes, sir," he replied, smiling proudly at Mr. Hinterlund, then shyly at Claira.

"Did your father make that for you?" asked Tressa, now pointing at the rustic cart.

"Yes, ma'am, well, actually, no. I mean, he made it for himself, truthfully," he explained and set about shrugging his shoulders and puffing his cheeks awkwardly.

"Why, it's lovely," said Tressa, smiling. Claira was smiling, too!

"My father died a year ago yesterday," he added while looking at the road and thinking it sounded much happier than he'd intended.

"Yes, we know," Magnus sighed solemnly before continuing brightly. "I knew your father, he was a genuinely kind and decent man, and well, we're all very sorry for your loss."

"It's kind of you to say so," said Deryn with equal parts pride and sadness.

After which an uncomfortable silence ensued until Tressa wisely changed the subject. "I believe you've met Claira before?" she enthused, recognizing a boyhood crush when she saw one.

"Why, yes, ma'am, although I doubt that she would re —"

"Of course I remember you, silly," interrupted Claira. "You worked at the fruit stand beside the butcher shop, remember? And I would always come in to buy a basket of —"

"Pears!" Deryn interjected with his brightest smile to date. "I'm honoured, I mean, it's an honour to be remembered, um, by you," he said and followed it up with more fidgeting and awkward cheek-puffing.

But Claira, who was gaining an enormous amount of pleasure out of his discomfort, simply laughed and said, "Silly boy!"

Even Deryn couldn't help but laugh in spite of himself. And as their eyes met on that freshly painted morning, he could've sworn he heard a small voice inside say, *She's absolutely lovely.* The next voice he heard, however, was that of the not quite as lovely Mr. Hinterlund.

"Well, young man, I s'pose we should be on our way," he said while exhibiting the same tight-lipped grin as before. "But we wish you all the luck in the world and look forward to seeing you again in the not too distant future," and gave his head a slight bow, though his face was now obscured by the sun in Deryn's eyes. And so, with a tip of his hat and a flick of the reins, they were off down the bright road toward town. Deryn watched them for a moment, and as they pulled away, he had but one shining thought in his mind. *Look back*, he said to himself. And she did!

In all of Hinthoven there was really no one to speak of who spoke French. Nor was there anybody who even spoke of French given the chance to speak of it. But if there were, they would most certainly know that the name Tourtière (roughly translated, at least) meant quite simply … meat pie. And strangely enough, to see him approaching down a narrow street could give one the impression that an actual meat pie was coming toward them. Roundish and pasty looking, he had the appearance of steam rising from his forehead at all times. Nobody knew where he came from, but then he didn't exactly invite inquiry into these matters. Truth be told, people mostly kept their distance. You might say he was an enigma wrapped in a misery. On one hand Tourtière was widely regarded as the best hunter in all the land, yet he was a strict vegetarian. His pleasure seemed to derive from the killing of animals, but not the devouring of them. He existed, rather, on a steady diet of potatoes, bread, and booze and lived a good staggering distance from The Fist and Firkin, where he dined nightly and always alone.

On this particular morning, Jacques had already reached his personal hunting quota for the day and so was preparing to head back into town when he heard footsteps approaching from up the path. And it wasn't very long at all before he could see just whom the footsteps belonged to!

"Hedlight? No, it can't be!" and chuckled menacingly. Now, like most bullies, Tourtière was not without a sense of humour. And like most bullies, this humour would mostly revolve around the humiliation of other, smaller victims. Tourtière hunched down behind a nearby bush and aimed his rifle toward our unsuspecting hunter. "BANG!" said the gun.

Deryn's heart leapt into his throat as he felt a hot breeze go whizzing past his left ear. Without hesitation, he dove for cover, landing headfirst into the nearest and most convenient mud puddle. Reality became momentarily surreal as he looked down and caught his reflection in said mud puddle. For the branches above had created the illusion of antlers sticking out of his head.

"Well, that's odd," said Deryn. "I'm a deer!" And he proceeded to laugh in a most beautiful and childlike way.

This whimsical daydream, however, would have to wait, for he was immediately brought to by the sound of Tourtière trudging up the path and laughing in a most awful and unchildlike way.

"Oh, Hedlight, it's you!" he said. "I thought you were a raccoon! Come to think of it," his cruelty continued, "you do sort of look like one with all that crud on your face."

Here he laughed again with the sort of mean-spirited laughter that ricocheted all around the forest and o'er the fields of Hell, presumably.

"You could've killed me!" shouted Deryn, his voice quivering with both anger and fear (though mostly fear).

"Now, if I wanted to kill you," said Tourtière with nary a trace of irony, "believe you me, you'd be dead," as he took a moment to survey Deryn's meagre accoutrements. "Just what do you expect to do with that gun and that, that sleigh or whatever you call it over there?" he chided dismissively.

Looking back on his simple tools, Deryn could find only one reason to come to their defense. "My father made that!" His voice broke with wounded pride.

Tourtière gave his head a pitying shake before adding his unsolicited two cents. "Hunting's for big boys, Hedlight. Maybe you should try fishing, or better yet, ballet!" and laughed cruelly once more before brushing past young Hedlight without even lifting a finger to help him up.

But after kneeling for the duration of this whole unpleasantness, Deryn wanted none of his help, anyway. And so picked himself up, happy in the knowledge that the terrible brute was gone at last. "Someday," he said under his breath (on the off chance that Tourtière was still within earshot), "he'll get what's coming to him." Then, standing at the edge of this curiously beckoning forest, Deryn gritted his teeth into a most determined scowl. "And with any luck, I'll be the one bringing it."

CHAPTER 4
HEDLIGHT GOES A-HUNTING

After a few hours of stalking the forest to no avail, Deryn was beginning to think maybe, just maybe, Tourtière was right. Perhaps he should take up fishing after all. Even ballet was beginning to look like the more realistic option by then. He wasn't at all sure if he had the heart or the stomach for hunting. At one point he even had an easy shot at a rather plump-looking hare, but decided against it after seeing she had little ones in tow. And feeling the familiar pangs of failure while still bearing the mud scars of his earlier humiliation, Deryn decided to rest awhile at the foot of an ancient tree. It felt good to lean on something that had withstood all of time's wrath yet remained standing. From this low place on the ground and from an even lower place in his heart, he began to feel quite small and insignificant. Not only in the eyes of the world, but especially in the belly of this eerily quiet forest. Looking up through the branches, he could see the outline of the moon as it prepared for its grand entrance. The sun, too, had commenced declining as the twilight did some of its finest work with the leaves and shadows.

But after a few moments of taking in all that beauty had to offer, Deryn broke free of nature's spell only to find that his life

was pretty much right where he'd left it. *I guess I had better start heading back,* he thought.

It would be dark soon and he did not wish to worry his mother more then she was prone to be. So using the tree for support, he backed himself up and off the ground to gather his things for the defeated hike homeward. T'was in the midst of all this gathering, in fact, when he heard a rustling from a bushy area off to his right. Deryn crouched low behind the same tree as before and reached for his rifle, which, as it turned out, was just slightly out of reach. In an effort to extend his arm further than was humanly possible, he soon found himself tumbling forward in a most ungraceful somersault with his back coming to rest hard on top of it. "Ooof!" he groaned and winced in pain. The pain, thankfully, would be short-lived, as it morphed mercifully into adrenalin. For from his new vantage point he could plainly see that something was indeed moving beyond those bushes! "A deer!" he assumed. "Well, that would certainly get us through the winter."

Deryn's mind drifted off momentarily as he imagined himself victoriously smoking his father's pipe. He could see his mother looking on proudly as she prepared a succulent deer stew for dinner.

Then, giving his thoughts a gentle shake back to the work at hand, he deftly rolled himself off the rifle and into a low firing position with it now pointing in the direction of the mysterious sounds. "How about that?" He smiled inwardly at this tactful manoeuvre. "Maybe I'm not so hopeless after all." Before long he began to zero in on some vaguely furry movement in the trees, only now it was much closer and ever more tangible than before. His heart was beating so loudly that at first he wondered if perhaps he'd mistaken IT for the sound of hooves approaching. But no, this was real all right. As real as the rifle that trembled in his hands. As real as the brave finger that set out alone toward the trigger.

"PLEASE," was about all he could say as he pulled back hard on it. "BANG" was about all the gun could say....

Time itself seemed to hang suspended for a spell as the forest circled all around him. For in the madness of that split second, the gunshot gave way to a high-pitched yelp followed closely by a milk-curdling scream! The unexpected blowback of the rifle, as well, sent poor Deryn tumbling backward into the muck for a third humiliating time.

And looking even more dishevelled then you would've thought possible, Deryn stood up slowly and felt around once more for his gun. As he did so, he did not lift his gaze from the place where the bullet had flown as, with a mad look of mud-caked confusion, he paused to wonder. "What on earth was that?"

CHAPTER 5

MEMORIES OF CRAD GRIMSBY

Crad Grimsby was born and roughly brought up in the town of Hixenbaugh. It was only a few miles, give or take, from The Willow Tree, where he had worked the better part of his life. Truth be told, all those who frequented the inn would be hard pressed to think of anything even resembling work that he did there — unless greeting travellers and prying into their personal affairs could be considered as such. In fact, there were two others on staff who, by all accounts, had taken on the lion's share of everything that needed doing while Crad chatted up the customers.

First and foremost was Gerty (a middle-aged woman, also from Hixenbaugh), who prepared the meals and made up the rooms, of which there were ten, and Charlisle the bartender and occasional bouncer who worked six nights a week and took Sundays off for devout reasons. So only on Sundays then, after Gerty had gone home, would Crad be forced to assume any of the aforementioned duties, not to mention the pouring of drinks or the serving of prepared food from a limited menu. (The dishes he'd always leave for Gerty to wash in the morning.)

Well, on this seemingly unremarkable day, as she arrived at her usual time, she would soon find that the normally cheerful Mr. Grimsby seemed unusually troubled, to say the least....

He'd not slept well, if at all, since the arrival of his most recent guests and their departure earlier that morning. And so, as he stared blankly out the kitchen window, it became apparent at a glance that all was NOT well and things were definitely NOT as usual. "Everything all right, sir?" inquired Gerty, to no reply. "Sir?" she gently repeated while setting down her bags and cautiously moving toward him. Still no response. "Mr. Grimsby?" she tried calling out this time while tapping his shoulder, which seemed to do the trick!

"Huh?" he blurted out, startled as if pinched by a ghost. His eyes were bloodshot and his hair was literally standing on end. "Oh, Gerty! It's you!" he gasped with hand over heart. "You know, you really shouldn't sneak up on people like that," he added (though clearly reassured to be seeing a familiar face).

"Is everything all right?" she attempted to ask him again with eyes that searched wildly for explanation.

"Yes, everything's fine!" he replied, though somewhat unconvincingly. He wasn't entirely sure he believed it himself! "I didn't sleep a wink last night," he further explained. "My mind, it just wouldn't shut off!" He laughed sheepishly.

"Well, maybe you should go have a lie down, sir," said Gerty. "I can take care of things down here, as you well know." Then, laying a motherly hand upon his shoulder, she couldn't help but notice that his shirt was completely soaked to the skin. "Mr. Grimsby! You're not well! You really should be in bed! Now you go right this instant and I'll bring up some tea," she scolded in the stern yet caring manner that he'd grown accustomed to.

"I'm going, I'm going," Crad chuckled groggily. "What would I ever do without you?" he wondered aloud while inching slowly toward the staircase. Gerty's eyes followed him every step until he arrived safely on the first landing, before she rushed off to fill the kettle. Once upstairs, though, he had barely enough strength to push open his chamber door before collapsing face down on his single bed.

"Those eyes," he sighed heavily. "Surely this can't be happening again." Grimsby rolled on to his back and looked up at the ceiling, which over time had become a virtual road map of cracks, chipped paint, and the occasional cobweb. On this day, however, all that could be seen in it was the face of his kid sister, Merthaloy, forever young and frozen in time, 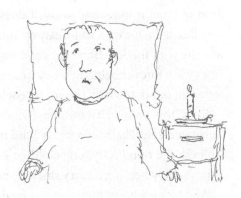 for she never got the chance to grow up. A flood of memories soon came rushing in from early childhood. For all that was too painful to remember had just now arrived to drag him back there kicking and screaming.

☙

He'd scarcely entered his teen years when his mother died suddenly of a suspicious illness, leaving Crad and Mertha to fend for themselves on the dirty streets of Hixenbaugh. It's safe to say that no brother and sister were ever closer than these two were during this difficult time. For the double hardship of a father who'd apparently abandoned them, only to lose their mother a year later, was some bitter medicine to swallow. Even so, they managed to survive and, indeed, thrive.

Crad took on odd jobs delivering milk and even digging graves, until before long he was able to afford a suitable room above The Lonely View Tavern for them both to live. (Come to think of it, it was not unlike the room he occupied now.) Merthaloy would wash dishes in exchange for food, which she always kept warm and waiting for him upon his return. You could say things were just starting to look up for our orphaned Grimsbys. But then life can be a cauldron of cruel ironies, and sadly, it doesn't take much for it to tip over like red wine on a white carpet. You see, Hixenbaugh's history was rife with folklore of witches and warlocks from a distant past. Tales were forever being told of evil spells and of how the witches were run out of town by the good people there.

Even the name *Hixenbaugh* (which roughly translated into German means "belly of a witch") did much to cement these dark fables in the minds of young children everywhere. For what child doesn't enjoy hearing a scary story? Especially at bedtime!

And Crad, who by then had assumed the tandem roles of father and big brother, thought it best to pass on these stories to Mertha and to advise her, as well, on all the many ways of knowing if you were in the presence of a witch to begin with. "First of all," he said to rapt attention. "You may notice a purplish aura around the pupils and a vague scent of candy floss and clay." Merthaloy's eyes were as wide as two moons as her mind raced to commit all this to memory. "Now, what you need to do if you even think you're in the presence of a witch is run! Run as fast as you can!" he whispered in a serious, yet loving, voice. "Their feet, you see, have these painful bunions on them, so they can't go very fast."

Mertha nodded and felt somewhat relieved to know that at the very least she was a fast runner!

"And one more thing," said Crad. "Witches and water DO NOT MIX! Now this is very important," he pressed on, his voice becoming more dramatic with each syllable. "For water to a witch's body is like FIRE, only ten times hotter! This is why you must ALWAYS carry 'round a flask of water!" (Here he paused to make sure she was still paying close attention.) "You do know why, don't you?" he asked mischievously as Mertha shook her head with the utmost seriousness. "'Cause you never know when you might get thirsty!"

With that he laughed merrily as she smiled a bright smile on the moonlit pillow and rubbed her sleepy eyes. "You get some rest, my angel," Crad softly said, "I'll see you in the golden morrow," and kissed her curious forehead before heading downstairs for his customary drink, or nightcap as he liked to call it.

Now, the following segment took place unbeknownst to Crad (for he had to work early that day), but it was later relayed to him by Sallee the innkeeper's wife, then pieced together from a few other eyewitness accounts. I should also mention that further liberties were taken by yours truly to fill in the gaps where dialogue was unknown and generally embellish the story for the purposes of this book ... you're welcome.

The next morning arrived like any other as Merthaloy woke rested and descended the staircase to wash a stack of breakfast dishes. As she did so, she would often look out the window that faced the courtyard. For she loved to watch the birds and squirrels as they worked tirelessly each day for survival. It reminded her of her big brother in the sweetest way.

Well, it was about this time that a woman's face suddenly (and quite chillingly) appeared in this very window. "Hello, there! What's your name?" asked the face.

"I'm Merthaloy," came her startled response.

"Merthaloy, you say? Why, that's a lovely name and for such a lovely girl, too!" said the window face, now smiling broadly.

Mertha backed up ever so slightly in an effort to check the eyes for any trace of purple. "What's YOUR name," she then asked suspiciously, and for good reason. For, just as she suspected, the eyes HAD come back positive for purple tint!

"Well, you're a bright child, aren't you?" said the purple-eyed lady. "You know better than to talk to strangers. That's very wise. Did your mommy teach you that?" she inquired and continued smiling, though her eyes did not.

"My mommy's dead," said Merthaloy flatly. Then, dunking a sly ladle into the dishwater, she splashed without warning a full load into the unwitting face of the witch, who screamed loudly as if burned by acid or scalding hot soup.

"You wicked demon!" she raged with a hole now in her cheek that one could practically see through. "You'll be sorry for that!" threatened the witch before ducking swiftly out of sight.

A moment or two later, Sallee the innkeeper's wife came rushing in to see what the matter was while looking frantically in all directions. "What is going on in here?" she asked with eyes wide. Mertha ran swiftly to her arms and pointed to the window, but alas, there was nobody there....

"What is it, dear? Whatever did you see?" implored Sallee, looking first at the empty window then back at the fully frightened child.

"A witch," cried Mertha. "I saw a witch!"

"Oh, come now," said Sallee. "They're just stories, you know!"

"But I saw her! She had purple pupils!" insisted Merthaloy, whose words spit out in a most adorable way. "I burnt a hole in her cheek!" she added while peeking out from under Sallee's arms and over to where the face used to be.

"Well, whoever it was, dear, she's gone now. I promise you!" For Sallee had this wonderful way of reassuring people with a comforting voice that Merthaloy, as well, had come to trust without question. "Why don't you run upstairs and collect yourself, and I'll have a look around ... okay?"

So as fast as her tiny feet could fly, young Mertha raced up the ten steps to her chamber and rushed over to the window. Which was exactly when she saw the witch again. Only now she was glaring upward at her from underneath a willow tree across the way, her face still smouldering from the dishwater wound. Her eyes still mad with rage. Her smile every bit as broad as before! Then in the blink of a purple eye, with fingers raised to the sky, she began the chanting of words that poor Merthaloy could not hope to hear from that distance behind the glass. (Nor would she have understood them even if she could.) After which the dishwater-disfigured woman simply turned and walked on, leaving behind her a sad space in the window where a little girl used to be.

People claimed that after her disappearance, they could still see her in the window most nights waiting for her brother's return. Crad himself would see her, too, and go rushing up the stairs only to find that she wasn't really there at all. It seemed she wasn't really anywhere anymore....

Most nights he'd spend looking over at the willow tree, imagining her sweet face on the pillow and praying for her to come home. But as with most prayers, it too went unanswered, and so he never did see her again. Not in the window and nevermore on the pillow. For it had truly become The Lonely View Tavern, as though it were predestined to be so. And as you've no doubt gathered by now, Grimsby would eventually leave the town of Hixenbaugh with all its heartbreak and never look back. Until very recently, that is.... But strangely enough, it was Merthaloy now who smiled down at his face on the pillow. Had she come to reassure him or to warn him of future trouble? It took but a soft rap on his chamber door to rouse him from his memories. "Tea's ready, sir!"

CHAPTER 6

IN THE CLEARING

They say that everything happens for a reason. More often than not, the reason becomes apparent only in hindsight. But hindsight, as we all know, waits on the brush stroke of time to show us the big picture and put our past in a frame. And certainly the scene awaiting Deryn in the clearing would make for one very sad painting indeed. For Jupiter lay dying, as seemingly unaware in death as in life, with Eleanoir providing what little comfort she could offer her friend. Deryn peered through nearby branches, the full weight of realization sinking his heart like a shipwreck. "Oh no," he gasped through fingers that covered all but his left eye. And setting down his guilty rifle, he pushed quietly through the brush and nearer to the tragic scene that lay before him. Approaching on foot, though, would prove much easier than approaching the right words. For what could he possibly say that would make any difference now?

He didn't wish to disturb the solemn moment, and, what with being the cause of it and all, words seemed especially meaningless and even harder to come by. Even so, Deryn removed his woollen cap, held it to his heart, and began to speak in earnest.

"Ma'am? I just wanted to say that it was I who ... well, you know, and I feel just awful about what has happened. I didn't mean to, of course, um, what I mean is, I thought it was a deer ... truly I did. And I really should have, well, I guess I just don't know how I could've been so ..." (and words to that effect), Deryn struggled on through real tears until finally arriving at the heart of the matter. "I just wish there was something I could do or say to show you how truly sorry I am," and hung his head in a genuine display of remorse.

Throughout the entirety of this heartfelt speech, Eleanoir sat hunched over the now lifeless body of Jupiter, and she neither looked up nor uttered a single word to acknowledge his meek presence. But now she turned at last to catch a glimpse of this remorseful dog murderer.

Her eyes did not seem at all wet from crying, though it appeared (at least to Deryn) that the twilight descending on the forest seemed to originate from somewhere deep within them. The unusual beauty of her face, as well, was unlike anything he'd ever seen before, and though he couldn't quite put his finger on it, something sure seemed odd about her! And much to his surprise, Eleanoir then smiled warmly at him in an effort to put him at ease, I suppose, though it had the opposite effect. "I believe you," she said, somewhat reassuringly at least. "It was just a mistake, I know. I can tell you're a good boy. You probably don't believe me, but I can tell." And she rose to her feet as though she were made of smoke and then fanned in his direction. "Jupiter," she said, now standing eyeball to eyeball with him.

"Jupiter?" he repeated, more than a little confused.

"The dog's name," she reiterated slowly, "was Jupiter."

"Oh, I see!" said Deryn, whose eyes seemed neither willing nor able to meet hers for even a second.

"Won't you be a dear and help me to bury him?" she then asked (and rather abruptly, or so he thought). "We must bury him quickly!"

Sensing that here, perhaps, was a golden opportunity to make amends in some small way, Deryn gathered up most of his wits to energetically rise to the occasion.

"Yes, of course!" he said brightly before running off to fetch a small shovel he had just remembered packing that morning.

"Now where the devil is he going?" wondered Eleanoir, craning her neck ever so slightly to the left. But in less than a heartbeat all became clear as he returned, shovel in hand, and got right to work digging a suitable grave for a beautiful dog who he assumed deserved much better. And as he toiled away with the best intentions, all the while digging himself a deeper hole, Eleanoir sat watching from a nearby stone and smiled unnervingly at him. Though he tried not to show it, Deryn was starting to feel a little put off, quite frankly, by how well she was taking it all.

"Would you like to say a few words, ma'am?" he inquired while tramping down the last shovelful of dirt on the grave.

"Words?" she asked. "What good are words at a time like this?" she berated him and cackled harshly. "He's dead, he can't hear us!"

"Well, I just thought," he said with a look of bewilderment unequalled in all be-wilderness. "That is, I mean, he *was* your friend! Well, wasn't he?" Deryn asked innocently before searching her eyes, but to no avail.

"Friend?" scoffed Eleanoir. "Oh, come now, he was a dog! A stupid, slobbering dog! Do you even know what a friend is?" she rudely inquired, all the while moving malevolently toward him.

"Well, no, I mean, yes, of course I do," he nervously spoke, now having become quite flustered by the whole situation. "I'm sorry, I'm just confused is all," he said, backing up slowly (for she was standing a little too close for his diminishing comfort). And also, he couldn't ignore for much longer how fast the night was approaching. "I-I really should be going," he stammered. "It's getting late, and my mother, well, she'll be beside herself with worry if I'm not home in time for supper."

At this Eleanoir glared, completely unmoved by this small dilemma. "I'm sorry to have caused you so much grief and pain," he added before turning and walking briskly in the direction of home. (Although he'd begun to wonder if she even knew what grief meant.)

"A deer, you say?" her voice rang out, stopping him in mid-stride.

"I beg your pardon?" he asked without facing her.

"I believe you said that you mistook my dog for a deer?" Eleanoir cheerfully interrogated him. "Well, did you or did you not?"

"Yes," said Deryn, sounding much less cheerful. "It's true, I mistook your dog for a deer. I don't know what else to say. It was all a terrible mistake. One I'm sure I'll regret for as long as I live. But now, I really must be going," and he continued on his less than merry way, this time with even more determination.

"Just an innocent mistake then, was it?" she mercilessly taunted. "Well then, what choice do I have BUT to forgive you?" she added with even more sarcasm and then laughed, which hardly seemed appropriate. Despite all her teasing, Deryn pushed on ahead, though with each step he could feel her twilight eyes burning a hole into the back of his brain. "You know, it's kind of funny," she continued. Her voice now sounded strangely musical, bringing Deryn's march to an abrupt halt.

"What could possibly be funny about any of this?" he snapped as Eleanoir moved in closer to where he stood on the path. "Personally," he said, his voice rightfully simmering, "I don't find anything amusing about this at all."

"Oh, really?" replied Eleanoir. "Well, you see, the funny thing is ... that I mistook you as well."

"What do you mean?" demanded Deryn. "You're not making any sense!"

"Then allow me to explain," replied Eleanoir calmly. "You see, at first I thought you were a man ... but you're not, are you? In fact, you seem much more like a deer to me, if I'm being totally honest," she said (while trying not to laugh at the bemused expression glaring back at her).

Deryn could not recall anyone ever trying his patience as much as this woman, but now she had truly gone and upset the apple cart! "You're insane!" he spat out in frustration. "What were you doing out here, anyway, with that enormous dog? Don't you know there are hunters in these woods?" He scowled awkwardly, which only made her laugh harder, as she buckled over in a fit of cruel mirth.

"Silly boy," she said upon regaining her composure, prompting a strange bout of déjà vu as Deryn, clearly perplexed, took a moment to recall Claira Hinterlund saying those exact same words earlier that morning!

But looking back, he noticed how Eleanoir's face had, in an instant, become as serious as the forest was dark. "You really are a deer, you know," she whispered, all the while biting her lip and nodding her head slowly, 'til all at once, with hands in the air, she began the chanting of strange words. A language, though, that the forest seemed to understand fluently. For as she spoke, it circled madly 'round him as an intense queasiness overtook his belly. In the next instant he began to heave violently and vomit in a most unholy way. Through it all, Eleanoir's laughter echoed down the corridors of his brain, shaking his very foundation until the life he'd come to know and love came to a screeching halt and everything went pitch black.

∽

When Deryn finally came to, he was all alone in the woods. And looking down into a completely different puddle from the one he had dove into earlier that day, he noticed yet again how the overhanging branches had somehow created the illusion of antlers. "I'm a deer," he said. Only now he had no voice. And there were no trees overhead.

The Fist and Firkin was hardly the place for a woman like Maggie Hedlight to be caught dead in. But Deryn had failed to make it home for dinner, so, as predicted, she was beside herself with worry. The only person she could think of who just might know something of his whereabouts was, of course, Jacques Tourtière. And this being his local and all, it seemed a logical place to start. Unlike most people in Hinthoven, Maggie wasn't the least bit afraid of Tourtière. She saw him as little more than an overfed bully long overdue for a smack in the behind from a wooden spoon. (Come to think of it, she had brought one with her just in case!) Maggie had passed by The Fist and Firkin on many occasions but had never ventured inside, nor would she have, if it wasn't such an urgent mission. The bar itself, having been built into the side of a hill with its main entrance situated in the wall of a bridge, was every bit as dark within as it was without.

There were always raucous noises and rough voices emanating from inside, and many a drunken brawl would ultimately crescendo with some poor soul crashing through a window and on to the street below (where, naturally, it would pick up right where it left off). This was in no way ideal for the neighbours who were trying to sleep, but for the local window maker, business was booming!

As she reached the entrance to the tavern and being of diminutive stature, she would soon find out that just grabbing a hold of the door handle would be a challenge in and of itself. But after she had bounced up and down a few heroically unsuccessful times, the door flew open seemingly on its own, unleashing a roar of commotion unlike anything she'd ever heard in all her days. For at that moment, a rather boozy-looking red-haired man was in the process of being physically ejected by a couple of bald bouncers wearing dirty aprons. So, taking advantage of this small window of opportunity, Maggie strolled in casually as though she were walking through her own front door.

Once inside the smoky din of The Fist and Firkin, she looked around in all directions until she spied what could only be the rotund silhouette of one Jacques Tourtière. He was sitting alone at his usual table with a bottle of brandy and a half-eaten loaf of bread. Without hesitation, Maggie made a beeline straight for him, which, as she would also find out, was much easier said than done. For just walking across the floor of the pub was akin to charging through a raging battlefield. Between the darkness and the smoke, it was next to impossible to get to where you were going without bumping into a table or two or tripping over a few bodies along the way.

Even so, brave Maggie sallied forth until she arrived safely at the place where Tourtière sat slumped over his umpteenth glass of brandy, mumbling to himself. "Mr. Tourtière?" she yelled over a chorus of rowdy conversation and positioned herself so that he might see her better through the haze. "Do you know who I am?" she demanded. Tourtière creaked his neck stiffly toward her, and she could've sworn she saw a flicker of recognition in those bloodshot eyes, but no such luck …

"Whoever you are," he growled, "you'd best hop on your broomstick and fly away," before returning sullenly to his thoughts (assuming he had any).

But Maggie was in no mood to take any lip from this toxic bully, so she pulled out her trusty wooden spoon and gave him a good whack across the back of his head! The force of the blow knocked the glass clear out of his hand as he turned to face

her with an expression of utter shock mingled with extreme rage.

"What's wrong with you! Are you mad?" he shouted while slamming his doughy fist down on the table.

"I asked you a question," said Maggie, completely unruffled by this outburst. "Do you know who I am?" she asked again calmly, then tapped her spoon on the edge of his table with menace.

But little did she know that a crowd had been gathering behind her ever since the commotion began. And Tourtière, who was not used to so much attention, thought it best to de-escalate the situation. "All right, I give up, who are you?" he asked as if going down to the cellar of memories but coming up empty-handed.

"Does the name Deryn Hedlight mean anything to you?" she inquired with folded arms and raised eyebrows.

"Hedlight?" He laughed dismissively. "Let me guess, you're his mommy and you've come to fight his battles for him? Then you're going to send me to bed without any supper, I s'pose?" This unlikelihood he finished off with a coarse laugh that segued into a violent coughing fit.

"Yes, I am his mother," Maggie replied. "But no, I've not come to fight his battles or send you to bed! I would just like to know if you saw my boy today … well, did you?"

At this question, Tourtière simply shook his head before cracking a most hideous smile. "I saw him, all right. That boy of yours had no business being out there with a gun. I wouldn't be surprised if he blew his own head off by ax-o-dent. Better off without it, if you ask me," he offered then proceeded to pour himself another shot.

"Well, do you know where he is now?" she continued, clearly disturbed by his careless attitude t'ward pretty much everything. "You didn't hurt him, did you?"

Tourtière threw back his brandy in a single gulp and peered sideways at her like a shark. "I was walking out of the woods" (here he paused to demonstrate by walking his fingers on the table) "and HE was walking in … end of story," he condescended as he refilled his glass once more without even looking at it.

"Well, if I find out that you've done something to him, I swear I'll …"

But before Maggie could even finish the thought, Tourtière grabbed hold of her scarf and pulled her face uncomfortably close to his. "I said END OF STORY. Now, if I were you I would leave right this instant before I throw ya outta here myself." The above sentence came spraying out through bearded lips and into her face in the most heinous way. His breath smelled of rotting teeth, damp socks, and ammonia. As for Maggie Hedlight? Well, she'd seen quite enough of Tourtière to last a few lifetimes (not to mention The Fist and Firkin), and so decided she'd be better off searching for Deryn all by herself.

With any luck, she thought, *he'll be waiting for me when I get home. Maybe he just got lost along the way.* She smiled inwardly with eyes that brimmed outwardly with tears. It was certainly within the realm of possibility, knowing Deryn. She mustn't give up hope!

So after mindfully navigating the minefield back to the front door, she was just about to head off into the night when the two bouncers I'd mentioned earlier in the chapter stepped right in front of her. Maggie looked up into their faces, expecting to find more trouble there, but was relieved to discover that the four eyes she met looking back down on her … were kind. "We'll help you look for him," they said.

CHAPTER 8

DEER FRIEND

As you can imagine, the events of the last day had taken our young Hedlight completely by surprise. He had hoped the hunting trip would change him somehow for the better, but this was an entirely different animal. A deer, to be precise! He would spend most of the first morning checking himself out in various puddles and streams while exploring the limits and potential advantages of his new-found anatomy. The shock of his current reality was matched only by his sudden desire to nibble on twigs, fallen leaves, and other bits of shrubbery that a day earlier would not have appealed to him in the least. When he wasn't busy doing that, he passed the time mostly worrying about his mother. For how was she to know what became of him? Not knowing would surely break her heart. He thought a great deal about the witch, too, for obvious reasons. He'd heard all the stories as a boy but never believed for a second they could even remotely be true. He wondered, also, if this spell was something he might just snap out of someday. But whenever he thought of that poor dog, it made him think, perhaps, he had got just what he deserved.

"It's funny," Deryn reflected figuratively and literally (for he was staring into a puddle even as we speak), "I came to these woods hoping to land a deer or some other creature. So why am I so guilt-ridden over killing a dog? And a witch's dog at that! For all we know it was twice as evil as her! Besides, is a deer not an innocent animal, too? Come to think of it, I *am* a deer, and I'm sure I wouldn't like it one bit if I was minding my own business and some fool came along and shot me for no reason." It was in the midst of all this reflection that he got the distinct feeling that he was being watched. And as it turned out, he was right! For another deer had been watching him, and for some time, apparently, from the other side of a narrow stream.

"Hello over there!" hollered Deryn, though with his mind, for, as he would soon discover, this was how all animals conversed. The other deer, however, chose not to "mind answer" him back, but only sniffed the air curiously before galloping off briskly. "Hey, where are you going?" Deryn called after him but to no avail.

A moment later he would find himself in hot pursuit, which proved to be an excellent way of test driving his new legs! For now he was hurdling over rocks and branches with ease while zigzagging in and out of whatever obstacles the forest set in his way, until, after an extended period of giving chase, Deryn finally caught up to the mystery deer. He was standing near a cave at the foot of a grassy hill, looking nonchalant. And strangely, neither of them was even the least bit out of breath! (I should also add that the following conversation takes place entirely via animal telepathy!)

"Oh, there you are!" said Deryn with what he hoped was a neighbourly grin. "Why did you run away like that?"

Tilting his head suspiciously, the other deer simply replied, "Because you were chasing me."

"Well, yes," admitted Deryn, "but that's only because, um, you ran away from me," and got back absolutely nothing in response. As this conversation seemed destined for nowhere, he thought it best to head off in a whole other direction. "So anyway, what's your name?" he asked, mostly happy to have someone to talk to.

"Name?" wondered deer number two with a look that could be best described as vacant.

"Well, you know, a name, as in … what do I call you?" Deryn elaborated, though all it produced was an even more vacant look than before. He was beginning to think he'd have better luck talking to the grassy hill! "For example, my name's Deryn, and you are?"

"Sorry, I'm not following you," replied the vacant one before pursuing his own line of questioning. "What's a Deryn? And what would I need a name for, anyway?"

To which Deryn, after expelling mists of frustration out each nostril, struggled to think of a reasonable answer to what was actually not such an unreasonable question. "Let's say," he proceeded with caution, "that I see you on the other side of a stream, like today. But you don't see me. Now, what should I holler, if I wish to get your attention?"

"Get my attention for what?" Old Blank Face replied, making Deryn contemplate running up the hill and throwing himself off it. Even so, he stepped up to the plate and took one last swing at it.

"How about this? Let's say, I call you …" (while noticing how big the other deer's eyes were compared with his own) "… Big Eyes!" he exclaimed proudly with great relief for having thought it up so quickly. "Does that work? Would it be okay if I called you Big Eyes?"

As for our newly christened Big Eyes? Well, his only response was to shoot Deryn a look that is universally recognized as pity. "If it makes you feel better," he said. "You're not from around here, are you?"

For the rest of the day they walked and talked of everything. Deryn shared with him all the harrowing details of his encounter with the witch and of Jupiter, too. He talked about his mother, his life as a human being (which Big Eyes didn't fully believe). He even tried telling a joke or two, all of which fell flat, making him wonder if every deer lacked a sense of humour, or just this dullard. Big Eyes in return gave Deryn the general lay of the land, as well as briefed him on all sorts of helpful deer tips, such as where the tastiest leaves hung down, and, most importantly, where the best hiding places were during hunting season!

"My mother was killed by The Round One," he said rather bluntly before looking up at the tranquil sea of clouds.

"The Round One?" inquired Deryn.

"He's in the woods almost every day … he's very round," Big Eyes replied and quite accurately.

"Yes, I know him!" said Deryn and shuddered at the very thought of him. "His name's Tourtière!"

"Well, he's The Round One out here, although I have heard some of the squirrels refer to him as 'Bear Droppings.'"

"Bear Droppings? HA!" Deryn laughed (well, in his mind at least). And soon Big Eyes had no choice but to join in. For even in the animal kingdom, it seems laughter can be quite contagious. *So he does have a sense of humour after all!* thought Deryn, who was only now beginning to feel a bit more at ease about his unusual predicament. It felt nice to have made a new friend, and heaven knows he needed one.

Just then, a shadow of concern passed over the face of each deer as Big Eyes visibly froze and then whispered, "Did you hear that?" Deryn, too, became quite still as he tried his new ears on for size.

"Is somebody coming our way? What do we do now?" he asked with anxiety renewed.

"Quick, into the cave!" said Big Eyes. "They won't see us in there!" Even though they'd just met, it was already clear to Deryn that whatever Big Eyes said to do was undoubtedly in his best interest. So as our burgeoning friends huddled in the darkness with nothing but the sound of their two hearts pounding, it wasn't long before a familiar voice could also be heard calling out in the wilderness.

"DERYN! IT'S YOUR MOTHER! HOLLER IF YOU CAN HEAR ME!! DERYN!!!!"

Every instinct compelled him to run to her arms, but he knew that would be a grave mistake. She would never recognize him, anyway, not in his current state. Instead all he could do was watch the heartbreaking spectacle of his mother going slowly past. Her face was, as always, the very picture of love and kindness. Following close behind her came the two enormous bouncers from the previous chapter. And although he hadn't a clue who they were, it was comforting at least to know she wasn't out there all alone.

"Oh, Ma," he sighed. "Sorry for putting you through this." First her husband gone and now her son. It all seemed too much to bear. And watching Deryn throughout the duration of this sad parade, Big Eyes had become completely transfixed by something small and shiny rolling down his new friend's cheek. "Deryn?" he asked curiously. "Is there a waterfall in your eyes?"

After a long day's journey, it came as a welcome sight to happen upon The Willow Tree just as nightfall descended. Maggie and her two travelling companions (whose names, incidentally, were Griff and Gruff) had plenty of time to get acquainted as they searched in vain for any sign of Deryn. And because the twins were men of few words and possibly even fewer thoughts, Maggie wound up doing most of the talking, which was completely agreeable to her. "Oh, I know this place!" she said, smiling upward at the faded sign. "My husband once stayed here on his way home from Hixenbaugh! If I'm not mistaken, he'd come from visiting a friend there who'd opened a bookshop. At least I think it was a bookshop," she concluded, before floating on the river of precious memories.

All the while Griff and Gruff looked down from on high with genuine affection for this kind lady who had treated them like they were her very own sons (which was by no means the sort of treatment they were used to). The next moment, however, their peace would be shattered by the sound of a full-blown bar scuffle in motion! Recognizing this all too familiar sound, Griff and Gruff immediately sprang into action, both rushing in to see exactly who was punching who. But once inside, it took little more than a glance to suss out the situation at hand. For two men (one with a bloody nose) swung blindly at each other as another man struggled valiantly to keep them apart while, in the process, finding himself on the receiving end of most of the blows. The human punching bag in the middle was none other than Charlisle the bartender, and peeking out from underneath the bar in an effort to avoid any stray punches was our very own Crad Grimsby, who, for good reason, was a bit too distracted to notice that three new customers had walked in.

Without any hesitation, Griff and Gruff stepped into the skirmish and proved to be an enormous help to Charlisle in his hour of need. They simply picked up the troublemakers, as Maggie had witnessed at The Fist And Firkin, and booted them on to the street as if they were little more than drunken footballs. Everyone in the tavern gave them a well-earned round of applause. Maggie applauded, too, with considerable pride for her bald chaperones who, in less than one day, had proven themselves more than worthy of her trust. And not surprisingly, it was Charlisle who was first to greet our new arrivals with arms outstretched for some enthusiastic handshaking. "Your timing's exquisite!" he said, smiling up at the impressive giants. "Now, could I interest you all in some ice-cold ale? On the house, of course," he kindly offered. An offer, you may have guessed, that was met with unanimous approval, for they were all quite parched after their long hike. Feeling it was now safe to step out from behind the bar, Crad himself soon ambled over.

"Greetings!" he said with a slight bow to Maggie, followed by a bigger one for her two companions. "Name's Grimsby, welcome to The Willow Tree!"

"Why, thank you, Mr. Grimsby. I'm Maggie Hedlight, and here we have Griff and Gruff." Her voice rang out cheerfully as she produced

a corresponding hand gesture for each introduction. "We've come all the way from Hinthoven!" she added while checking his face for any sign of astonishment at this amazing feat of endurance.

"You don't say!" said Grimsby. "Hinthoven? I should think you must all be close to collapsing!" (To which all three nodded in the affirmative.) "Well then, why don't we go take a seat by the fireplace?" he kindly invited with his customary "wizard arms" fully extended.

Little did they know that they would be heading over to the same cozy nook where just a couple days earlier Eleanoir and Jupiter had enjoyed some respite before their own dark journey! Before long, Charlisle came rushing back as promised, carrying a tray of cold complimentary ales, and all three sipped gratefully and heaved sighs of relief for the simple luxury of sitting down.

"Did you have an early start?" Grimsby asked Maggie with a smile that was returned in kind.

"Why yes, we headed out this morning and have been walking all day," she replied with a knowing wink in Griff and Gruff's direction. "Haven't we?"

"Well, I hope you don't mind me saying so," Crad went on, "but you do seem, at least to my eyes, to have quite the unusual entourage here! Am I correct in assuming that these two strapping young lads are ... your sons?"

"Ha! No, they're not *my* sons," replied Maggie, clearly amused by the assumption. "Although I will say this! They've been so kind to me today that I may end up adopting them before too long." She giggled for what seemed like the first time in ages. (Though Griff and Gruff seemed much less enthusiastic at the prospect of this arrangement.) "To be honest with you," said Maggie as Crad listened on, "these nice boys were helping me search for my son today! His name was, I mean is, Deryn."

Grimsby turned to the twins and nodded his approval at them. "That's mighty kind of you, boys. Chivalry's alive and well, I see!" he remarked before bringing his full attention back to Maggie and wondering whether she might be of a similar vintage as him.

"He's been missing since yesterday," she continued, brushing away a small tear. Then, looking up, she began to search the inn-keeper's eyes curiously, for they seemed to share a similar sadness with hers. Within them she felt she could detect a certain shat-tered shop window of loss only a mother (or perhaps a big brother) would know of....

"I'm sorry to hear it, ma'am," his heart sighed. For a new and more disturbing thought had just now entered his mind. A thought, however, he was not at all comfortable sharing! "Your boy, was he in the woods, by any chance, when he went missing?" Grimsby delicately inquired while imagining purple eyes and thinking it was all much too sinister to be mere coincidence.

"Why, yes, he'd gone hunting for the day," replied Maggie, "I never should have let him go," and began to sob into the sleeves of Griff, who then held her in an awkward embrace.

Crad's mind had become inflamed with so many discomfort-ing thoughts that he began to feel positively faint. And noticing this sudden change in him, Maggie collected herself in an instant and confronted him on the spot. "Mr. Grimsby? Is something the matter?"

"Just a bit dizzy is all," he meekly replied while shuffling slowly toward the staircase.

Maggie rose from her chair and called out after him. "You've seen him, haven't you? Tell me the truth!"

Grimsby had not gotten very far when he stopped and turned to face her. "Ma'am, I swear to you, I have not seen your boy," he said without deception. "I'm afraid all the excitement of tonight's rumble has upset me more than I originally thought. Or p'raps it was the soup." He smiled (though it was more of a wince) in a weak attempt at lightening the mood. But looking into her eyes, his heart over-flowed with the following words. "I do hope you find your boy. You have no idea how much. But sadly, I don't feel so well at the moment. So I'm afraid I must bid you all a good evening. Please stay on as my guests and order whatever you like. It's all on the house!"

This he spoke with as much energy as possible under the circumstances before gesturing toward the bar. "Charlisle here will see to everything. Won't you, Charlisle?" he said, glancing over at his faithful barkeep (whose left eye, incidentally, was quite bruised from its earlier pummelling).

"Aye, aye, Captain!" came that man's jovial response.

As he climbed the stairs, so, too, did Maggie's eyes, as Gerty's had done just a day earlier. But upon reaching the first landing, he paused to look down, shaking his head sadly with eyes that strained to tell her all that his words were at a loss to explain. *He knows something*, thought Maggie. Though she wasn't at all sure if her heart was strong enough to know what it was.

And as the night pulls back its camera on our little inn at the edge of the forest, we leave Maggie by the fireside, her thoughts lost in a whole other forest of worry, with Griff and Gruff on either side like gargoyles on a cathedral ledge. And Grimsby on his single bed looking up at the face of Merthaloy, who'd been appearing nightly ever since Eleanoir first showed up. "You know something, don't you?" he whispered to the ceiling.

Her face seemed to nod, but then he wasn't sure of anything anymore. "Oh, Mertha," he sighed before rolling over to blow out the candle, which flickered at first, as if it, too, were afraid of the darkness fixing to swallow them both.

CHAPTER 10

BEAUTIFUL MORNING

Winter came as usual with its unwanted package of hardships and then left without a word of goodbye. But now, with spring in the air, it was time for all living things to "come out, come out wherever you are!" Deryn had stuck pretty close to Big Eyes throughout the difficult season, only to emerge triumphant as he stepped out to greet the morning sun. Everywhere he looked, life was either waking up or thawing out while unearthing a buried treasure of sights, sounds, and smells. All that had been barely perceptible to him as a human came into sharp focus in the most intense and emotional way.

"What are you doing?" asked Big Eyes with his dozy head poking out of the cave.

"I'm just ..." (here Deryn took a moment to gather the perfect bushel of words) "... taking it all in," he explained, swaying his head back and forth in lieu of hand gestures.

"Taking all what in?" Big Eyes wondered with much concern. "Whatever you plan on taking in, we don't have room for it in here."

Deryn shook his head and laughed. "No, you big hat rack! I'm talking about NATURE ... you see?"

But noticing how his friend's dimly lit expression remained unenlightened, he thought to give it another try.

"Look," explained Deryn, "when I say I'm taking it all in, what I really mean is … I'm experiencing it ALL with ALL five of my senses. Now do you see?"

"Five senses?" inquired Big Eyes suspiciously. "And where did you get those from?"

"Where did I get them from?" Deryn repeated with mild annoyance. "Why, the same place you got them. We all have them, you know!" (Big Eyes looked back at the cave to see if perhaps he'd left his in there.) "No, that's not it," said Deryn "I'm talking about sight, sound, smell, touch, taste. FIVE SENSES." (And stomped his hoof down for each of the five.) "Now do you get it?" he asked with understandable trepidation.

"Oh! Why didn't you say so!" said Big Eyes, grinning with relief. "Just keep them out here is all I'm saying," he continued, clearly not grasping it in the least. "We don't have room for all your senses, let alone mine in there!"

It seems our deer friends had become dear friends over the course of the long winter months. And aside from the occasional mind-numbing conversation, Deryn couldn't recall ever having a better pal, and he was quite certain the feeling was mutual. From Big Eyes's perspective, he'd been on his own for so long, operating on basic instinct, that he'd forgotten ever having a brain in the first place! Mostly he was thrilled to be getting some use out of it again. For every day Deryn would come bursting with questions and/or theories, all of which invited contemplation and made his small brain throb with activity. As for Deryn, although he missed his mother terribly, he was determined to make the best of the situation and live his life out to the fullest without any whinging if possible.

This being the first day of spring, our deer friends walked in golden silence, enjoying the warmth of the sun-dappled trees but mostly enjoying each other's company. All winter long Deryn had been lugging around a delicately heavy question and thought now was as good a time as any to set it down.

"So, were you there when The Round One, well, you know?"

"Do you mean when he shot my mother?" asked Big Eyes.

"Yes," said Deryn before adding, "I completely understand if you'd rather not talk about it."

Big Eyes looked to the sky momentarily before responding, "Yes, I was," though without any noticeable trace of emotion.

"I'm so sorry," Deryn offered. "That must've been just terrible. I mean, if anything bad ever happened to my mother, I know I would be devastated."

"I don't know what that means," said Big Eyes flatly. "But yes, I imagine you would be … def-a-stated, that is," and loped on ahead in silence. Deryn watched him as he walked away, not wishing to intrude in his time of reflection. Though truthfully, it was hard to tell if there was much, if any, reflection going on.

Just the same, he couldn't help feeling a little nosey for bringing it up. For although Big Eyes had not offered much in the way of details, he got the sense that it was still a very painful subject to address.

Upon returning to the day ahead, he was amazed to discover that while lost in thought he'd been missing out on the generous banquet Mother Nature had laid out before them. From this scenic vista atop the grassy hill, Deryn could literally see for miles. The trees below and river beyond all trembled with life 'neath a powder-blue sky. Birds, too, were flying around and singing all the songs he'd heard as a boy, only now he could finally understand what they were singing about! (He had hoped the lyrics would be better, though!) And turning to the east, he could even spy the old Hinthoven sign that stood ever faithful on the edge of his beloved hometown. "This is Heaven." He smiled inside 'til his heart was fulfilled enough to spill over with gladness.

But then, from out of nowhere (where most bad things originate), a loud pop was heard as something hot pierced his side. All four legs buckled under him as he collapsed to the ground in shock and in pain.

"Deryn!" shouted Big Eyes, as he came rushing back and looked down on his friend with grave concern. "Are you going to die, too?" he asked, helplessly eyeing the wound.

Deryn let out a weak moan while attempting the least convincing brave face in all of history. "I think it only grazed me." He smiled (though it was more of a wince) in a weak attempt at lightening the mood. Soon the crunching of footsteps could be heard approaching from the base of the hill. "You'd better go," said Deryn anxiously.

"I'm not leaving," came the predictably stubborn reply.

"Listen to me, you have to go!" Deryn insisted. "Or he'll kill us both!"

Big Eyes shook his head all the more defiantly, making Deryn all the more upset. "GET OUT OF HERE, I SAID. GO!!!" his mind rightfully screamed, sending a tree load of birds scurrying across the sky.

But as the footsteps drew nearer, Big Eyes relented and reluctantly turned to leave. He'd not gone very far, however, before Deryn called out to him one last time. "Wait!" And as Big Eyes waited, eyes soulful and sad, Deryn created lines hopeful and glad.

"I just wanted to say thank you for everything. It may not have been a very long life, but it has been a sweet life, and the best part of it was knowing you!" he spoke straight from his heart and then nodded as if to say, "That'll be all."

So after taking one last look at his wounded comrade, Big Eyes gave his head a hopeless shake and sped off into the woods just as man and rifle were seen coming around the bend. "Well, I guess this is it," said Deryn, presumably to the sun, with eyes full of wonder and tears as he heaved a

sigh of gratitude for everyone he'd ever loved in his relatively short life. In doing so, he could feel his troubles ease into the warm bath of a peaceful dream as all fear and sorrow became wrapped mystically in grace. "At least I got to have this one last beautiful morning."

CHAPTER 11

OUT OF THE WOODS

he old Hinthoven sign had undoubtedly seen better days, though it is doubtful it ever felt less lonely than it had of late. For Maggie Hedlight had made it her daily constitutional to head out there each morning, rain or shine, ever since Deryn went missing. She had truly not given up on her son, despite the fact that many people in town had begun to question her overall sanity. Positioned at the crossroads where the forest begins and the countryside ends, the sign had been performing the thankless task of greeting visitors, farmers, and hunters for ages upon ages. (Though they never did get many visitors, if we're being honest.) Somewhere along the way an overbearing tree had decided to wrap itself around the sign, obscuring a

few essential letters in the process. Not that anybody seemed to notice, for it had read NTHOVEN for about as long as folks could remember. Next to the sign there lurched a rickety old fence that was every bit as faded as the sign itself. On top of this fence sat Maggie Hedlight, legs dangling, with Griff and Gruff leaning in on either side. And all three staring wistfully at the forest.

Maggie believed to her soul that someday Deryn would emerge from there unharmed. For to believe otherwise was just too dark a thought to entertain. Little did she know how close this dream was to coming true, and right before her eyes! For in the distance a horse and cart was steadily approaching with two figures sitting up front. If her eyes had been working better, she would've recognized them instantly as Magnus and Claira Hinterlund, though it wasn't very long at all before their familiar faces came into relatively sharp focus at last. Then, as Maggie waved warmly at them, she also noticed how the wagon they were pulling carried a deer inside. A deer that was still moving!

"Ah, Mrs. Hedlight!" said Magnus with a tip of his hat before acknowledging Griff and Gruff with a look of curiosity and horror.

"I see you have a live one there?" exclaimed Maggie, obliviously pointing at her own son.

"You can thank Claira for him," sighed Magnus, shaking his head. Claira flashed a bashful smile at Maggie, followed by a loving one at her father. "How could I say no to those eyes?" he wondered aloud while shrugging helplessly. "I was just about to put the poor fellow out of its misery when this here young lady came to the rescue!"

Maggie's jaw dropped before looking over at Claira, who could only nod sheepishly back at her. "But why, dear?" she asked with mild astonishment. "That one could've fed the both of you all month!"

"I don't really know why, Mrs. Hedlight," replied Claira. "There was just something about him. It was almost as if … he recognized me!"

Magnus then winked at Maggie. "Truthfully," he said, "it was Claira's first hunting trip," while nudging her playfully and added, "quite possibly her last! She hasn't the spine for it, I'm afraid."

A melancholy shadow passed over Maggie's heart in remembrance of her lost boy. "It was Deryn's first hunting trip, too," she said, looking down as the Hinterlunds gave each other a solemn sideways glance.

"We're really sorry about Deryn," offered Claira. "We saw him at this very spot, in fact, on the day, well, you know, the day he went …"

Maggie's eyes brightened in anticipation. "You saw my boy?"

"Yes, ma'am," said Claira, turning to her father, who nodded as if to say, "Go on." "Well, we were on our way to town," she continued, "and he was walking toward us …"

(Here Claira's voice trailed off as the sadness leapt into her throat.) "He was a fine boy," interjected Magnus. "In fact, I think Claira took quite a shine to him, didn't you, Claira?"

(Now, this nugget of personal information, under any normal circumstances, would've no doubt horrified young Claira. But after seeing the pleasure it brought to Mrs. Hedlight, she decided to elaborate on it in her own words.)

"He was very sweet," said Claira. "But I feel a bit guilty now because, well, you see, I was teasing him a little that day. Not in a mean way, though."

"Aw, don't worry yourself about it, dear," said Maggie. "He spoke of you often! You made quite an impression on him, I dare say," and grinned absent-mindedly before continuing.

"You'll probably think I've gone mad. A lot of people already do, but I believe he'll be back. I just have to believe." Maggie then teared up suddenly, as Claira, who had already begun crying, hopped down from the wagon and ran straight to her arms. Soon there were moist eyes all around. Even on the faces of Griff and Gruff.

As for Deryn, from his position strapped down in back of the wagon he couldn't see much of what was going on, but he could certainly hear and feel it. In fact, he had never felt so many conflicting emotions in all his life!

On one hoof, there was this feeling of relief at being spared by Claira's compassion. On another hoof, not being able to tell anybody who he was felt miles beyond frustrating.

"So, what do you plan on doing with him then?" Maggie wondered, looking back over at the wounded deer.

"Well, Father thinks we've only grazed him," Claira replied optimistically. "So we're going to nurse him back to health, right, Father?" To which Magnus could only sigh and shrug his shoulders.

"We're going to try!" he said. "I'm sure Tressa will know what to do. She always does!" Then, raising a mock scolding finger to her face, added semi-seriously, "But if or when he gets better, it's back to the woods for him. Understand? He's not a dog, you know!" After which he commenced tousling her hair, forcing Claira to giggle and squirm desperately before breaking free of his loving clutches.

All the while, Maggie looked on with feelings that were filtered through her own playful memories of her boy. The bittersweet expression on her face spoke louder than any words as the merriment faded into the sad reality.

"Well, I suppose we should get this beast home and see if we can fix him!" said Magnus. "It was nice seeing you, though, Mrs. Hedlight, and we sincerely hope that you find your boy."

"And I won't forget to keep him in my thoughts and prayers," added Claira, making her father more proud than even he thought possible.

"You know, it's funny," said Maggie, "but just running into you like this, I can almost feel his presence." (As Deryn pricked up his ears in the background.) "It's almost as though he were here listening to everything we're saying and knowing how much we miss him," she further explained, then finished off with an expression of peace so contagious that even Griff and Gruff appeared much more like angels and much less like bouncers.

Magnus, though, could only look on sympathetically (and maybe even a little skeptically, truth be told). "Well, 'til next time," he said doffing his hat to the twins.

As they pulled away, the wagon slowly loped past Maggie until she was able to catch a closer glimpse of the wounded deer and was awestruck, too, by what she saw. "I think Claira was right!" she called out to the back of the Hinterlunds.

"Right about what?" asked Magnus, looking over his shoulder.

"I think this one here recognizes me as well!" She smiled and shook her head as Magnus winked and Claira waved goodbye.

But then, looking into the deer's frightened eyes, her face softened as only a mother's can as something deep within her heart compelled her to say the following words: "Don't be afraid. These nice people will take good care of you. Do you understand?" But then to her utter amazement, the deer's head bobbed up and down as if understanding her completely. This seemingly mystical interaction left Maggie in the road with her mouth agape as Griff and Gruff looked on, greatly moved by what they had witnessed. And lo, from yonder hill, another set of eyes had been watching them all intently for some time now. "Def-a-stated," he said to no one.

CHAPTER 12

CRAD'S BIG DAY OUT

Throughout the winter months, Crad Grimsby had time to think about a good many things. He'd thought a lot about the witch and her dog, which was to be expected. And although he had tried to forget the past and at times even Merthaloy, he found remembering her to be much more beneficial to his over-all peace of mind. Mostly, though, his thoughts were of Maggie Hedlight and her missing boy. He couldn't help but think there was a connection. Some invisible thread, perhaps, that strung them all together. To put it plainly, he was a lonely man and wondered if she just might be lonely, too. He didn't know her age offhand — it would've been rude to ask — but he had the feeling that it couldn't possibly be too far off his own. Her face, which had not left his memory since the night they first met, held a certain kindness that tugged at his inner child and was, at this very moment, in fact tugging him toward Hinthoven!

Grimsby had set out on his woodland march earlier that morning dressed in his Sunday best and leaving The Willow Tree in the capable hands of Gerty and Charlisle. The ever-thoughtful Gerty had even packed him a generous lunch of cucumber baguettes, pears, almond butter cookies, and a flask of wine to help brighten his journey. (All of which he had consumed within the first ten minutes!)

Well, just a half an hour from town he was, and moving along at a pretty good clip, when his foot met with some immovable object, catapulting him through the air and tumbling ox over plough down a steep embankment, lastly into a fresh pile of bear droppings. "OOF," he groaned 'neath an audience of convulsing trees. "What the devil?" he wondered while rolling himself over and back on to his feet again ... which took some doing.

Then, looking up from below, he could see at a glance the most likely cause of his tumbling.

Now, if falling down the embankment was easy, then clawing his way back up to the path seemed at first impossible (for a man of his age and circumference, at least). Fate, happily, would prove merciful that day. For it took only a few false starts before he was seen panting and wheezing back to where the slapstick tragedy had begun.

And so it was, after much grunting and groaning, that Grimsby finally rose to his feet while brushing himself off as best he could. His "Sunday best" looking more like his "Monday worst," he couldn't help but laugh in spite of himself. "Not exactly the impression I was hoping to make." He chuckled and wiped his brow with a faded handkerchief.

Then, looking down from above, he could clearly make out P. Hedlight carved into the side of an old rustic cart!

"Well, I'll be," he said with hand thoughtfully placed on chin. And although the cart, which had been stuck in the mud and frozen in place all winter, seemed at first impossible to excavate (for a man of his age and circumference, at least), luck happily would also prove merciful that day. For it took just a few hard yanks before he had freed it from its earthly grip and none the worse for wear. "So where's the boy?" he wondered to himself while perusing his immediate vicinity.

But then, noticing a small clearing in the trees that seemed worth investigating, he soon found himself tiptoeing through a maze of branches with both eyes fixed on the ground.

And it wasn't very long, either, before he stumbled upon Deryn's rifle, too, right where he'd set it down that fateful autumn day.

"Wonderful!" said Crad, now feeling like a sort of amateur sleuth. But as he bent down to retrieve the rifle, a dark wind circled up and blew through his thin hair like a comb. And to his horror, on the bark of an old twisted tree, the face of Eleanoir suddenly appeared! Recognizing her immediately, Grimsby shrieked loudly, dropping the rifle, which in turn discharged, causing him to leap and then dive for cover into a nearby bush!

But after a few moments of cowering, Crad tentatively poked his head out, only to find her face still glaring back in all its menacing glory. "What do you want from me?" His voice shook with fear. Next time he looked, however, the bark began to morph into that of another face he instantly recognized. "Mertha?" he gasped through a web of trembling fingers. "Is that you?"

His sister spoke not a word but looked sadly at the foot of the tree. With astonished eyes he followed her gaze down until they arrived at what appeared to be a shallow grave. A grave, he feared, that must certainly contain the body of young Deryn Hedlight. "No!" he gasped. "This is all so terribly sad!"

Kneeling beside the humble mound, Crad moved his hands over the dirt as he began to pay tribute to an unlucky boy, who much like his own sister, never got the chance to grow up. "You were a good boy, weren't ya?" he offered, not really knowing what to say. "Your mother loves you, of course. In fact, she hasn't stopped looking for you! I don't expect she ever will." He sighed before continuing. "Well, I'll be seeing her very soon, and I just want you to know that I have your things. Your gun and your cart. I'll make sure she gets them … you can count on me."

With that Crad rose stiffly until he stood over the grave and honoured Deryn with a moment of silence. The faces of Merthaloy and Eleanoir had faded, much to his relief.

And what with the daylight fading, too, he quickly gathered up all of Hedlight's belongings and headed back to the trail that would ultimately spit him out of the woods and on to Hinthoven in the springtime. But what a grimy-looking Grimsby it was that emerged as the sun submerged beyond the meadow. And unbeknownst to him, he was leaving it in much the same way that Deryn had entered it! Carrying the rifle and even pulling the cart Pearson Hedlight had cobbled together once upon a time. It seems they had more in common than either one could've ever imagined. Upon reaching the tree-wrapped NTHOVEN sign, Crad took out a pocket knife to cut away a few of the imposing branches until it hailed HINTHOVEN again for the first time in ages. "There," he said, clearly pleased by his untapped pruning abilities as he limped toward the sleepy candlelit town of Hinthoven now flickering in the distance, "that's much better."

whole calendar page had been flipped over since Deryn first arrived at the Hinterlund farm. As expected, Tressa had lovingly attended to his wound, and, what with it being a superficial one, it had healed beautifully into a thing of the past. His new life with Claira was more joyful than either one ever dreamed. For one was seldom seen without the other, and though she'd always dreamed of having a horse of her own, nothing could turn the curious heads of the Hinthovians more than the sight of young Claira Hinterland riding into town on a deer. She had just turned sixteen, and though it took some persuading at first, her father had not only agreed to let Deryn stay on indefinitely but had even consented to the occasional trip into town, providing they were home before dark. Claira felt light as a feather on Deryn's back, and it was with enormous pride and precaution that he squired her about the town.

Even the shops of Hinthoven had all but adopted them as local celebrities. The bakery, for example, always saw to it that Deryn got a special treat of his own and fresh water to drink. Her favourite dress shop even tied a colourful green bow around his neck (which he wasn't at all convinced suited him). But no trip into town would be complete without first checking in on his poor mother. Claira never fully understood how this tradition got started, but she loved it just the same. For she could plainly see that somehow a deep connection existed between Mrs. Hedlight and Lucky. (Which reminds me, Lucky's the name Claira gave to her pet deer!)

As for Maggie, she greatly appreciated these visits and always looked forward to them. For other than Griff and Gruff, nobody ever really stopped by. This was all about to change, though, and sooner than she or anyone else expected! "Would you like more tea, dear?" asked Maggie as Deryn curled up in his usual corner.

"Yes, please, it's the most delicious tea, Mrs. Hedlight!" remarked Claira in all honesty.

"Why, thank you! You know Deryn could drink a whole pot all by himself!" Maggie fondly remembered. "And afterward he could fill the whole chamber pot!" To which both laughed merrily.

T'was in the midst of this merriment when there came a light rapping on the front door. Maggie glanced at Claira in astonishment, as though some miraculous event had just occurred. "Now who could that be?" she asked, looking at Lucky, who appeared to shrug with uncertainty.

"Only one way to find out, Mrs. Hedlight!" said Claira. "Answer it!"

Maggie moved sprightly to the door and squinted through the peephole. "Well, I'll be!" she said, hastily unlatching the chain and pulling open the heavy wooden door. "Why, Mr. Grimsby, as I live and breathe!" she said, clearly startled by this unexpected visitor.

Grimsby poked his comical face in through the doorway, first winking at Claira, before producing a visible double take at the sight of a deer in her living room. "Oh, you have company," he said. "I can come back later if —"

"Nonsense, Mr. Grimsby," Maggie interjected. "I may not have the biggest house in town, but I can certainly fit one more in here!"

she enthused, patting him on the back and helping him out of his overcoat. "Claira, I'd like you to meet Mr. Grimsby!" she said, just slightly out of breath from wrestling with the aforementioned overcoat. "He owns a charming little tavern on the other side of the woods called The Willow Tree!"

"It's lovely to meet you," replied Claira with an even more charming curtsey.

"And this here's our special friend, Lucky!" continued Maggie, who could not recall ever having so many guests at one time.

"Well, he must be special," said Mr. Grimsby, who could not recall ever seeing a deer indoors before, as he knelt down (with great difficulty) to give Lucky a pat on the head just as he had done with Jupiter not so long ago. "You're a good boy, aren't ya! Yes, you are!" he said before rising (with even greater difficulty), yet somehow managing to park himself on a low tuffet near the fireplace. Deryn's old seat, to be exact!

"So what brings you to Hinthoven, Mr. Grimsby?" Maggie inquired as she poured him a fresh cup of tea.

"Please call me Crad," he replied. "And, well, to be honest, I've come to see you," he said with a flirtatious wink.

"You have?" said Maggie, looking back at Claira with even more astonishment than before. "Well, I'm flattered, but why come all this way to see an old bird like me?" she asked, genuinely mystified as Claira beamed back at them as if it was the most adorable thing she'd ever seen.

"I'm afraid it's somewhat of a private matter," Crad explained, nodding first at Claira, then over at Deryn, who, to his astonishment, nodded right back at him! "Well, you see," he said, looking once more at the unusual deer before continuing, "on my walk here, I literally stumbled upon a few things that I believe may have belonged to your son."

Maggie raised a hand to her lips and gasped. "Well, anyway," he cleared his throat before proceeding, "I'm staying at The Fist and Firkin, do you know it? It's just around the —"

"Know it? I wish I didn't know it!" interrupted Maggie with no small amount of scorn before adding, "Now, Mr. Grimsby, I mean Crad, there's a lovely bed and breakfast not too far away that would be much more suitable than that godforsaken place." She fumed while recalling her own unpleasant experience there. "You would like it!" and jabbed him in the chest hard with her finger.

"I don't doubt it," said Grimsby. "But you see, I've been sleeping above taverns my whole life. It's where I feel most comfortable. Sad but true," he explained and then smiled at the ground help-lessly before resuming. "Well, like I was saying, I found these items, you see, I would've brought them with me, but I wanted to see you first ... to talk."

"Whatever did you find?" wondered Maggie, her mind rac-ing with both hopeful and fearful thoughts. Deryn, for his part, was pretty sure he knew what it was Grimsby had stumbled upon, but as he looked over at Claira, she was now rising from her chair.

"I suppose we should be going, Mrs. Hedlight," she said, stretch-ing her arms up to the ceiling. "We'll give you two a chance to get caught up." A considerate gesture to be sure, as Grimsby nodded and smiled back appreciatively at her.

"Well, if you must, dear," said Maggie, now rising to give Claira the warmest hug, which never failed to make Deryn smile inside. "But thanks ever so much for stopping by. And please, give my best to your father, won't you? He's such a wonderful man!"

"He is indeed," replied Claira before turning to Deryn. "Go on, Lucky, say goodbye to the nice lady!"

Maggie gave him a kiss on the snout and whispered, "You're my special friend, you are. Now you get this lovely girl home safe, you hear?" To this modest request, Deryn simply nodded as if to say, "But of course!"

"This one here understands everything we say!" Maggie chuckled and shook her head. "I've never seen anything like it!" The peculiar traits of the deer sent Maggie and Claira into fits of girlish laughter. Grimsby's face, though, seemed more troubled and less amused.

He's like no deer I ever saw, he thought and wondered if witchcraft just might be involved. And so, after this sweet round of goodbyes, Claira and Lucky were soon heading for home as the sun crouched down into the fields. Like Maggie, Claira could see in Lucky this unique ability of not only understanding her but also of conveying whatever he was feeling. It was as though they had their own secret language.

These were the thoughts occupying her mind as they rode out past the crossroads and on to the countryside. Deryn's thoughts, however, were all of his mother, Mr. Grimsby, the found items, and whatever else they might be discussing back in town.

As they reached the farmhouse, the sound of soft crying could be heard coming from behind a stoic tree. Claira immediately hopped off and stepped lightly toward the source of the sadness. "Tressa? Is that you?" she asked while peeking 'round the tree trunk. And clearly surprised by this delicate ambush, Tressa was forced to collect herself as quickly as she could.

"Oh, it's you!" she said, wiping away a tear and attempting a smile. Claira couldn't recall ever seeing Tressa so upset, which made it all the more upsetting.

"What is going on here?" she asked in a fresh panic. "Why are you crying? Is Father okay?"

"Yes, he's fine. Don't mind me," Tressa insisted. "I'm just being foolish."

"I don't understand," said Claira. "Where's Father?"

"He's inside, but please don't tell him you saw me crying, please!" Tressa implored, clutching her shawl with both hands.

Claira backed away slowly in a fog of confusion before turning, then running toward the house. And Deryn, who was feeling every bit as unsettled, followed close behind until both disappeared through the back door, which slammed shut like a heavy textbook.

"Father!" Claira called out fearfully.

"We're in the kitchen!" he hollered back cheerfully.

We're? thought Claira and Deryn in unison. And as they raced to the hallway just outside the kitchen, another voice could be heard mingled in with that of her father. Deryn could've sworn he recognized it from somewhere, but before he could give it any more attention, Magnus himself appeared in the hall to give them both a welcoming hug. (Which was unusual in and of itself!)

"Is everything okay, Father?" asked Claira with concerned eyes.

"Yes, everything's fine," he replied and laughed for no apparent reason.

"Have you been drinking?" she demanded. "You're scaring me!"

"Haven't touched a drop," he said, grinning mischievously. "But I have met someone!"

"You've met someone?" repeated Claira. "But who? And how?" (Wondering if it had anything to do with Tressa's tears.)

"You're not the only one who went into town today," he playfully spoke. "In fact, I looked everywhere for you, but you were nowhere to be found," he added with mock suspicion. "Where have you been all day, Miss Hinterlund?"

"Well, we went to visit Mrs. Hedlight," answered Claira as if in a trance. "She and Lucky have really hit it off."

"Is that so?" said Magnus. "And how is our Mrs. Hedlight?"

"Um, she's fine, but Father," her voice now lowered to a whisper, "whoever did you meet?"

"Right! I almost forgot!" he said while providing a rare glimpse of the pearly whites behind his trademark grin. Then, taking her by the arm, he led Claira into the kitchen as Deryn began to immediately buck and bleat with the utmost distress. Disturbed by this unexpected reaction, Claira looked over at her best friend with eyes full of fear before turning at last to meet her father's mystery guest.

"Claira Hinterlund," he announced with an exaggeratedly formal air, "I'd like you to meet the lovely, the enchanting Miss Eleanoir."

CHAPTER 14

HEDLIGHT HOME

We now rejoin Maggie and Crad getting reacquainted over tea. Lucky and Claira had just left for home, leaving behind a space that could only be filled by shy glances and awkward bits of conversation. "She's a lovely girl!" said Maggie, fidgeting with her hands and looking up at the ceiling.

"She is indeed!" replied Crad, scuffing his feet and looking down at the floor. "And that deer is quite something, too," he added before reclaiming his low seat in the corner.

As he did so, Maggie dragged her chair to the farthest reaches of her tiny living room so as not to appear overly flirtatious. It seemed like ages since she'd been in the company of a gentleman caller, and so she couldn't quite recall what the proper etiquette might be. "Ever since I met that deer, Lucky, I've felt strangely comforted," she further explained. "As you can imagine, it's been quite a challenge just getting my hopes up every day, ever since Deryn went missing. But whenever I see Lucky … up they go!"

Crad smiled and sipped his tea, which slurped much louder than he'd intended. "Mmmm," he enthused, looking at his cup as though it held the answer for it tasting so good.

"So these items you mentioned?" Maggie inquired. "You say you stumbled upon them?"

"And how!" said Grimsby, chuckling at the memory of it. "One of them sent me rolling, quite ungracefully I might add, down a very steep incline."

"Oh my! Were you hurt?" asked Maggie, who upon closer inspection did notice a few rips and tears in his apparel (not to mention some curious stains).

"I'm fine, really, Maggie, all things considered," said Grimsby. "I come blessed with extra padding!" (Here he performed a brief paradiddle on his overflowing belly to demonstrate.) "Except for these torn clothes and some wounded pride, I think I came out of it rather well!" he laughed while inspecting one of the many scratches on his lower arm.

"So what was it that caused such a tumble as that?" asked Maggie, not finding any of it amusing at all.

"Well, it was a kind of a sleigh-ish contraption, with wheels and a handle for pulling," Crad replied, checking Maggie's face for any sign of recognition. "There's an inscription on the side that reads *P. Hedlight*, which I'm assuming is …"

"My husband!" Maggie spoke up excitedly. "You found his hunting cart!"

"Yes, and what I believe to be his rifle, as well. I have them back at the inn."

"But no sign of Deryn?" she asked with hands folded in prayer.

"I'm afraid not," he replied, though with considerable guilt. He had debated telling her about the grave but decided against it at the last minute. "If you like, I can drop off his things tomorrow," he said to no response, for her mind had just now drifted off somewhere.

"Maggie?" He gently talked her back to the present.

"Oh! I'm sorry Mr. Grim — I mean Crad," she responded, slightly embarrassed. "My mind, it tends to wander these days." After which she took a long sip of tea before continuing. "But yes, you can bring it all over in the morning. I'll be here."

Only now it was Grimsby's turn, for his mind had wandered off, too! It wandered over all the parallels between his sister's disappearance and that of Maggie's missing boy, though he couldn't decide if telling her about Mertha would be a help or a hindrance. He thought, as well, of the witch and even the unusual deer in Maggie's living room. But not knowing how to broach any of these subjects, he decided instead on raising a whole other one.

"I wonder if I might ask you about your late husband?" he delicately inquired.

"Yes, of course," said Maggie. "What would you like to know?"

"I'm just curious to know when and possibly how he passed away," he replied.

"Well, it's going on two years now," she recalled and glanced toward the front door, where a black bowler hat hung on a rusty nail. "That hat there's what killed him," she said, to his amazement.

Crad scanned the hat curiously before bringing his eyes back to her. "I'm afraid I don't understand," he said, looking once more at the hat, which seemed innocent enough.

"Well, you see, he had just returned home from visiting a friend in Hixenbaugh."

"Why, that's my hometown!" Crad interrupted excitedly.

"Is that so?" replied Maggie. "Well, come to think of it, Pearson did say he had stayed at your charming inn once on his way home." This added greatly to Grimsby's gobsmacked expression.

"He did?" Crad wondered aloud while placing both hands on his head as if to pull out what little hair he had left. "Why, this gets stranger by the minute!" he then declared and shook his head in relative disbelief.

"Do you remember him, by any chance?" she inquired. Crad's smile faded to give his mind a moment to tackle this question.

"Hmm." His thoughts went rummaging 'round in his brain before finally arriving at the definitive word on the subject. "No," he said. "I can't place him. I meet so many people, you see. But please continue."

"Well, as I was saying, he'd just returned home from Hixenbaugh and was all excited about this new hat he had just bought," she went on to explain and pointed her teacup accusingly toward the door. "That hat! He told me he'd purchased it from a lady with purple eyes! Can you believe it?"

But Grimsby, who was in mid-swig as this information was being relayed, began to choke immediately, before spraying an impressive tea geyser out both nostrils like a whale.

"My word, Mr. Grimsby! Are you all right?" she asked, now thoroughly dripping with second-hand tea.

"Yes, Maggie, go on, I'm listening," he said and pulled himself together as best he could as Maggie watched him curiously for a moment before continuing.

"So anyway, Pearson was all a-flutter about this new hat, which I found quite unusual. He was never one to get excited about things in general. He was very even-keeled, you see?" Then she nodded at Grimsby, who wondered if he himself could ever be described as even-keeled. "Apparently she told him this sort of hat would not blow off in the wind!" she scoffed and rolled her eyes dismissively. "Well, it was not long after that, he and Deryn were out picking up a few things from the market, when from out of nowhere a gusty wind kicked up and blew the hat clear off his head!" Grimsby sat on the edge of his seat as she went on to explain what happened next. "Now, I wasn't there, but according to Deryn, the hat blew on to the street and around the corner, forcing my Pearson to go chasing after it like a stubborn fool," Maggie explained, now shaking her head at the indignity of it.

"Is there anything sadder than a man chasing his own hat down the street?" Grimsby wondered aloud while raising a philosophical question for which he assumed there was no answer.

"Well, sadly," said Maggie, "there is…. You see, he chased that ridiculous hat right into the path of an oncoming carriage!"

"No!" gasped Crad, already dreading the answer. "Trampled?"

"I'm afraid so," said Maggie. "The only bit of good news is that Deryn never actually saw it happen. Although he did see the aftermath," she ended on a solemn note and then finished off her tale of woe by looking back over at the hat. "That's all I have left of him now," Maggie sighed. "Heaven knows why I bother keeping it around."

"Oh, Maggie, I don't know what to say," offered Grimsby, whose mind had grown heavy from so many different thoughts, and all of a disturbing nature! He was beginning to feel a little queasy, as well, and felt it might do him some good to have a lie down. "Well, I've taken up enough of your time today," he said, quite shaken by all he'd been made privy to. "I s'pose I should be off," he said before adding at least somewhat cheerfully, "I'll be back, though, in the morning with those things I mentioned."

Maggie was feeling a little overwhelmed herself from the retelling of her husband's death. Not to mention all the emotions that are bound up with the receiving of guests and the relinquishing of them. So many hellos and goodbyes to speak of in a life of opening and closing doors. And as they rose to give each other a comforting embrace, words seemed unnecessary in the presence of their two hearts pounding. For it's times like these when a sigh will often more than suffice.

Soon Grimsby was back out in the fresh air and marching back to the stale air of The Fist and Firkin with more trouble on his mind than he could ever recall. A whole sea of humanity passed by him, though all went completely unnoticed. That is, until he reached the entrance of the tavern, where he came into contact with another man who was at that very moment exiting with great haste.

This unforeseen bodycheck sent Crad hurtling backward to the street below as he looked up and saw for the first time the steaming girth of one Jacques Tourtière, who scowled and then snarled at him. "Watch where you're going, idiot!"

CHAPTER 15

FROM BAD TO WORSE

f thunder be the drum roll for lightning, then Hinterlund farm had existed in a state of perpetual anticipation ever since Eleanoir showed up. You'd think the clouds had bought up all the sky real estate and built their own subdivision. Meteorologists and theologians alike could not recall such peculiar weather in all their days. And doomsayers were quite literally having a field day! So much thunder yet no rain or lightning.... No one quite knew what to make of it. If only they knew that this curious "anti-storm" had been brewing, at least figuratively, from within the very farmhouse itself. It had been just over five months since Magnus first met Eleanoir. Whether by some unlucky coincidence or by cruel design is uncertain. (Although my money's on cruel design!) It is now known that she'd been living there for some time doing God knows what and basically lying low.

At any rate, if love is blind, then Magnus Hinterlund's heart was now in total darkness. And as for Claira, Lucky, and Tressa? Well, each one of them felt quite helpless in the face of these dark changes. This once happy home, it seemed, had become veiled in shadow. A shadow only three could see through, for Magnus was too much in love to see what havoc this relationship had wrought.

In the first two months, for example, Eleanoir had persuaded him that since she'd be living there now, Tressa's services would no longer be needed. So after sixteen faithful years, she was unceremoniously let go.

Alongside the gaping wound her absence created, this once tidy and efficient household soon fell into disrepair. (And don't get me started about the cooking!) Tressa, though, felt strangely relieved by the sudden firing. For she had been in love with Magnus, and not so secretly, for years. But then oblivion knows no bounds, and she could no longer bear to be in that house any longer, though she missed them all terribly. The whole atmosphere, in fact, had begun to feel more like atmos-fear, especially for Deryn, who knew but couldn't say who or what they were dealing with.

Since Eleanoir had moved in, he was forced to sleep out in the barn due to her supposed allergies, which Claira didn't buy for a second. Eleanoir even recommended having him stuffed and mounted, and took great pleasure in frightening him at every turn with threats and knowing glances. And to make things infinitely worse, hasty wedding plans had just been announced to take place on the first day of September. Just two days away by my calendar! As you might've guessed, this unexpected development upset Claira to no end, and so on this very occasion ... she told her father as much.

"I can't understand why you'd ever marry such a horrible person!" She confronted him in the front yard and without even knowing the half of it! "It's like she's got you under her spell or something."

"Now, Claira," said Magnus. "You're not being fair. You want me to be happy, don't you?" he implored, now holding her face in his hands.

"Yes, of course I do, but with her?" she despaired, pulling away from him. "She's awful! She frightens Lucky terribly, *and* I can't believe you would ever let Tressa go!" Claira scolded while searching his eyes to see if he was still in there somewhere. "She was my best friend!"

"Is that what this is all about?" asked Magnus, glancing curiously at the clouds before continuing.

"Look," he sighed. "Tressa's a big girl, and she understood why we had to let her go. She was my friend, too, you know," he explained, though to the back of her head as he fumbled for the right words. "For the first time since Mother died, I'm happy, can't you see?"

"You don't know anything about her!" Claira shot back at him. "You don't even know her last name!" she said and burst into tears.

Magnus held her awkwardly for a moment as he struggled to express his feelings, which was never his forte. "When we're married," his tongue tiptoed cautiously, "her last name will be Hinterlund, and that's all that matters."

But Claira was in no mood to hear such things, and so violently pushed her father away, screaming, "I HATE YOU!" before running off in tears to fetch Lucky. Poor Magnus was helpless to do anything but watch as his daughter came bounding out of the barn atop the best friend she ever had as she galloped off in the direction of town.

A moment later, Eleanoir, who, as usual, had been secretly listening in to the whole exchange, came floating up behind Magnus and wrapped her arms around his waist. "Let her go, Mags," she soothingly spoke. "It's a lot for her to take in, but she'll come around. Trust me."

But Magnus was in no mood, either, to hear such things. "Leave me alone," he snapped, peeling her arms away and storming into the house as the door slammed even

more angrily behind him. This outburst, however, did little to rattle Eleanoir as she stood in the yard watching daughter and deer grew smaller in the distance. She was tired of running from town to town, from a small-minded world that had never, nor would ever, accept her kind. Whatever bad things she may have done along the way seemed almost justified in her twisted mind. Especially after witnessing first-hand her mother's relentless struggle to fit in, which brought only heartbreak, madness, and death. But that's another story, meant for another time.... You see, Eleanoir was a survivor, and at last she could see a light at the end of a very long tunnel. By marrying Magnus, she wouldn't have to run anymore. By wearing his name, she would someday be the owner of his entire estate.

But then Eleanoir wasn't the sort of person who waited around for "someday." And once these two troublemakers were out of the picture, she could finally be rid of Magnus, as well. "Or wait, perhaps the other way around?" she pondered and then nodded in agreement with herself.

For a new and ever more sinister plan was at that moment being hatched in her fertile mind. The very thought of it made an almost childlike grin break out across her face. Well, almost.... If you didn't know it, you'd think she was like any other blushing bride looking forward to her big day, and I suppose in her own way she was. *Poison apple?* she thought and chuckled deeply in her throat. *No, that's been done.* "Oh well, I'm sure you'll think of something when the time comes."

CHAPTER 16

AUGUSTAFEST

Despite the gloomy efforts of the sky, there was really nothing that could dampen the spirits or get in the way of the annual August Festival, or "Augustafest" as it was widely known. On the last three nights of August, the Hinthovians would celebrate the transition from summer into autumn with food, music, and, of course, vast quantities of beer. But since the mood at Hinterlund farm had not exactly been festive of late, both Deryn and Claira had completely forgotten all about it. The outgoing mélange of oompahpah music created a surreal soundtrack that was at odds, to the say the least, with their decidedly less than oompahpah spirits.

"Augustafest!" said Claira. "Is it the end of August already?" This question she posed to Lucky, who responded with an uncertain shrug. "Oh right," she said upon remembering her father's fast-approaching wedding date and then bristled at the thought. But as they moved slowly through the crowd of revellers, Deryn's thoughts returned to a much happier time. He could see his mother and father dancing to a bright waltz as he clapped along on the sidelines. He could taste the apple cider, the cinnamon buns, and smell the smoke of the bonfire all over again. Come to think of it, he could smell it all now, even as we speak!

"Look!" said Claira. "It's Mrs. Hedlight and Mr. Grimsby!" Deryn peered through the smoke to where scores of happy couples danced with wild abandon, and sure enough there they were. Never had the phrase *mixed emotions* ever seemed more appropriate than at this moment. For just the sight of his mother prancing around with another man filled him with much confusion. At the same time, a whole other feeling had begun to shed light on his wounded heart. A feeling he would later come to recognize as acceptance. This Grimsby character seemed harmless enough, and besides, it had seemed like forever since he'd seen his mother looking so happy. How could that be wrong? For unbeknownst to even yours truly, Crad had been making biweekly trips to Hinthoven for the sole purpose of courting Maggie Hedlight. Their friendship, or so it seemed, had blossomed like an awkward flower into a sweet companionship. It appeared they had much in common, even though he had yet to tell her about Merthaloy, the witch, or even her dog.

Nor had he mentioned the forest grave he'd happened upon. "Why break a heart that life's already broken?" was the question he forever posed to himself. While in town, he could often be seen accompanying her to the Hinthoven sign, along with Griff and Gruff, of course. (Although he wished they would just stay home from time to time.) And much to Maggie's unending disapproval, he continued renting the same room at The Fist and Firkin. "I'm a creature of habit," he would say. "Too late to change me now!"

Watching Mrs. Hedlight and Mr. Grimsby dance brought a smile to Claira's sulking heart, in turn helping her to forget her troubles for awhile, and in doing so, went a long way in easing Deryn's troubled mind, as well! It was in the midst of all this spinning, in fact, that Maggie looked over and saw Claira and Lucky standing on the outskirts of the crowd and enthusiastically waved them over. Before long, they were swept up in the swirling joyfulness of the dance as the crowd formed a wide circle around them and clapped along to the rare spectacle of a dancing deer. (Though to call it "dancing" might be a bit generous of me; he was definitely hopping around a fair bit!)

Well, after a few energetic polkas, our four unlikely friends decided to take a stroll away from all the noise and they cut through the cemetery that rolled on down to the peaceful river. Along the way, they even stopped at the gravesite of Pearson Hedlight for a moment of silence. After which Maggie remarked to the small congregation, "You know, it's strange! I always have trouble finding the stone, but not Lucky! He led us right to it! Didn't ya?" She shook her head in disbelief. Grimsby, who was now more certain than ever that this was no ordinary deer but rather a boy in deer's clothing, winked at Lucky, who as expected winked right back!

And as they reached the far side of the cemetery, Maggie and Crad took a seat on a thoughtfully placed bench overlooking the river while Claira and Lucky sat under a tree looking up at the sky. It was getting close to suppertime, but she had no intention of going home now, if ever. The wedding was just two days off, and since she had seemingly no power to stop it, all she could think of was running away. But where could she go?

"I thought I'd see your father there tonight," said Maggie, unaware of any family strife at home. "I used to love watching him dance with your mother. Poor thing, she was so beautiful! You're so much like her, you know!" she remarked before looking back at Claira, only to find her eyes now overflowing with tears. "Claira? What's wrong?"

Grimsby rushed to her side and held her as she deeply sobbed. (Deryn, for his part, could only nuzzle the back of her arm reassuringly.)

"Whatever's the matter, dear?" Maggie tried asking again. Though with all the heaving and sobbing, it was next to impossible for Claira to say anything at all. It would not be long, however, before she had composed herself enough to form actual words.

"Father's getting married in two days!" she spoke through her distress. Maggie and Crad glanced knowingly at each other as if understanding in a heartbeat what the matter was.

"Now, Claira," said Maggie. "Your father's been alone for such a long time. Surely enough of it has passed for him to —"

"You don't understand," interrupted Claira. "She's a terrible person! He barely even knows her!" she cried and then buried her face in her hands.

Maggie wasn't quite sure how to proceed at first but soon found her footing. "Is it possible that she's not as bad as you think?" she offered hopefully. "Your father's an intelligent man. I can't imagine he'd ever marry someone who didn't have your best interests at heart. Can you?" she endeavoured to hearten her while placing a gentle hand on Claira's shoulder.

"That's just it!" said Claira, inadvertently pushing her hand away. "He's not himself. It's like he's under a spell!"

But Maggie didn't know what to make of that remark at all. (Crad, though, was pretty sure he knew what to make of it!) "This woman," he spoke up tentatively, "does she by any chance have a large dog with her?"

"No," replied Claira. "Why do you ask?"

"Oh, it's probably nothing," he replied as Maggie watched him, looking even more perplexed by this odd question.

"Do you know this woman, Crad?" she asked to no response, for he was busy framing his next question.

"Her eyes," he continued. "Did you happen to notice what colour they are?"

Claira moved in closer and tilted her head curiously. She did seem to recall they were an unusual colour but had not given it much if any thought until now. "Purple," she blurted out after a moment's consideration. "At least I think they were purple," said Claira, who then eyed Grimsby suspiciously, for she had begun to think he knew more than he was letting on. (And judging by his reaction to this info, he most certainly did!)

For as soon as the word *purple* fell from her lips, Grimsby commenced a crumbling to the ground in a shivering, quivering heap. "Crad!" Maggie cried as she knelt down to put her hand on his feverish forehead. "What is it?" she pleaded to no response.

But thankfully it wasn't very long before he, too, was able to form actual words, though his voice now had become little more than a whisper. "Claira, you mustn't go home," he croaked as Maggie looked up just in time to catch Claira's newly horrified expression being born.

"You know who she is, don't you?" Claira spoke calmly at first before working herself into a fit of frenzy. "Who is she? What does she want? Tell me!"

"Claira, please!" implored Maggie. "Can't you see he's unwell, dear?"

Realizing that she had been a little hard on ol' Grimsby, Claira backed off immediately to give them both some much-needed space. "I just need to lie down," he said with a sigh. "If you'd be so kind as to walk me back to the inn, I promise to explain everything in the morning." He smiled weakly on his pillow of grass as Maggie looked down with love and concern (much like the face of Merthaloy).

So it was, after much heaving and pulling, that Maggie and Claira (with the help of Lucky) were eventually able to resurrect our fallen Grimsby until he was back amongst the vertical again. And although he improved greatly on the walk back into town, Maggie could not shake the feeling of dread that had just entered her mind. *Purple eyes?* she thought and wondered if it could have anything to do with the mysterious bowler hat, or more specifically the woman who had sold it to her late husband! "I must get rid of it," she said and made her mind up to do just that the following day.

As for Claira, she had more questions than ever, and so having to wait until the next day for answers would be like waiting for some evil version of Christmas to arrive. Deryn, though, couldn't help but feel a shade of relief in knowing that the witch who'd caused all this havoc might finally be revealed at last!

Upon reaching The Fist and Firkin, Maggie attempted once again to dissuade Crad from staying there. But as usual, he simply swatted the suggestion away. "I'm fine here, really I am." (Just as two men came crashing through the front window!) Grimsby, though, looked only mildly embarrassed by the timing of his last remark. "Let's say we meet at Maggie's tomorrow at one?" he continued, unfazed, to which all in attendance nodded in agreement.

"Now, is Claira okay staying with you tonight?" he asked while pressing his hand affectionately in Maggie's.

"Yes, of course," she replied and then blushed in a way that took years off both their faces. "She's welcome to stay, and so are you!"

"I appreciate the invite, Maggie, really I do. But as you know, I am but a lowly creature of habit," he said and sent them on their way amid the boozy oompahpah music, sounding much less cheerful now and more demonic, or so he thought, as the Augustafest band played on. "Thanks for walking me

back!" he called after them, looking and even sounding more like his former self. Maggie turned to blow a kiss in his direction, which he happily caught and placed in his front coat pocket.

Soon Grimsby was climbing the creaky steps up to his chamber, feeling greatly lifted by the kiss Maggie had directed his way as he began to hum an old childhood tune. A tune he could've sworn he'd heard Merthaloy singing once upon a time: "Leaves in the whirlwind, scarecrow's clappin'/All good children ought to be nappin'."

"Now what was that song again?" he wondered as he struggled to dig the bulky room key out of his front pocket. And in doing so, he dropped it with a loud clang. Soon he was down on all fours, cursing underneath his breath, and feeling around in the dark hallway, until he felt what could be instantly recognized as someone's boot!

"Looking for this?" came the eerily familiar voice of Eleanoir with eyes that practically glowed in the dark. And in the shadows behind her lurched the bulbous outline of Jacques Tourtière! (Known only to Crad as the rude person who'd knocked him down the stairs.)

"Ah, my key!" exclaimed Grimsby with feigned levity. "I would've been crawling around all night looking for that." Crad rose stiffly until he was once more at eye level with Eleanoir, as before at The Willow Tree. "Now, if I could just have that key," he said, "I'll bid you both a good night and put myself to bed." He spoke steadily while reaching out with trembling hand.

"Nonsense, Mr. Grimsby," said Eleanoir. "It's Augustafest! Why, you can't go to bed just yet! Especially after my friend here has invited us back to his place for a nightcap. Surely you're not going to pass up an invitation like that?"

Grimsby, who had the distinct impression that this was less of an invitation and more of a direct order, reluctantly complied.

So with Eleanoir and Jacques on either side of him, he was swiftly and silently escorted out of the dank tavern and down the dark alley toward Tourtière's foreboding abode. And as they marched along as if in a funeral procession, Eleanoir threaded her arm through his and chirped as though they were the best of friends. "Mr. Grimsby," she said, "I can't wait to hear what you were planning on telling our Little Miss Nosey-lund! Not to mention that old hag you've been seen around town with lately." Grimsby winced at the cruelty of her words and stole a quick glance at her face, which was briefly lit up by lamplight. Not surprisingly, it was every bit as unnerving as on that first night they'd met. "Oh, and by the way," she continued with a thinly veiled smirk, "you remember my dog, don't you? Jupiter? Well, anyway, you'll never guess how he came into my life, or for that matter, who that pesky deer is! It's a small world, Mr. Grimsby. A very small world!"

CHAPTER 17

THE GATHERING GLOOM

he thing about witchcraft is that it is by no means an exact science. In order for it to work at all, it must first be fuelled by some rage-induced event or by emotional upheaval of another kind. (As in the case of Merthaloy throwing the dishwater or Deryn's accidental shooting of Jupiter.) Even so, the spell must first have some significance to the unlucky soul it has been cast upon. For example, since Deryn had mistaken Eleanoir's dog for a deer, she was able to change him into one. And since Merthaloy was last seen looking out of a window, what better place, then, to keep her suspended in a nightmare from which there was no waking. Although it remains to be seen what Pearson Hedlight ever did to deserve such an unlucky bowler hat as the one Maggie was just now disposing of in a bin up the street.

As she laid it on top of the trash, it occurred to her that she'd never really looked at it all that closely before. It seemed ordinary at a glance. Upon second glance, however, she found herself positively transfixed by it. For sewn into the charcoal-coloured fabric were small flecks of purple that gave it a strangely hypnotic glow. Turning it over, she was even more intrigued to find a mysterious inscription on the inside that read:

C.O.W. Hixenbaugh.

COW? thought Maggie with a comically puzzled look. *Now what's that s'posed to mean?* Little did she know that the inscription had once stood for Coalition Of Witches.

AND NOW A BRIEF HISTORY OF C.O.W.

Around the time the hat was made, there came a small order of witches who'd all secretly moved back to Hixenbaugh in the hopes of infiltrating and ulti-  mately taking back what they believed to be their rightful home. By selling these hats, scarves, and pies, all with these purple flecks in them, they had hoped one day to unite their powers and summon up a tidal wave of black magic strong enough to wipe out the enemy.

(The enemy being the descendants of those who'd burned their ancestors at the stake and all those who ran them out of town with their torches blazing.) Fortunately for the good people of Hixenbaugh, this tidal wave of black magic was never to be. For the ringleader of C.O.W. was nabbed for questioning after a child noticed traits in her that were consistent with the bedtime stories she'd heard. This very public arrest sent witches scurrying like mice in all directions to avoid the police dragnet in full force. (One of these witches, you may recall, fled for Hinthoven at the outset of this book with a dog named Jupiter!)

After contemplating the meaning of C.O.W. for the entirety of the last paragraph, Maggie shook herself back to reality. Then, after taking one last look at the cursed hat, she said, "Good rid-dance!" though under her breath, for an elderly couple had been watching her and scowling with disdain at the disgraceful sight of a grown woman talking to a garbage can. Maggie waved to them in a friendly manner, though all she got back was a look that said, "Do not engage her." "Some folks' garbage is too good for the bin, I s'pose," she said before heading home to where Lucky and Claira were still awaiting Grimsby's arrival.

As she re-entered her humble abode, Maggie double-checked the rusty nail on the wall to make sure the bowler hat was truly gone before turning to her guests, who shook their heads in unison.

"Still no sign of him, eh?" she said, unwrapping her copious scarf. "What could be taking him so long?" she wondered aloud while looking up at the clock. It was already half past three, yet still no word from Grimsby.

"Maybe he overslept?" Claira offered hopefully. "He did have quite a stressful night, after all."

"True," said Maggie, who then shuddered anew at the thought of it. "I'd almost forgotten about that."

"What do you suppose brought that on?" asked Claira. "I mean, all I said was purple."

Maggie had debated telling her the story of Pearson's death by hat but decided against it. "I really can't say," she replied and then reached for a cold piece of toast on the table. "I was hoping Mr. Grimsby might shed some light on that very question!"

As she crunched in the awkward silence her bread, Claira and Lucky sat in the awful silence of dread.

For they were equally troubled by the imminent wedding, as well as Mr. Grimsby's disappearance. "I have an idea!" said Maggie as she washed down her toast with a swig of tea. "What if I were to take a stroll over to The Fist and Firkin and see if he's about?" she offered while scanning their faces for any traces of disapproval.

"Are you sure?" asked Claira. "Would you like us to come with you?"

"Thank you, dear, but that won't be necessary. My friends Griff and Gruff will be there, so I'll be fine, I'm sure of it. Besides, you should probably stay here in case he has taken some alternate route and we miss each other on the way. You know how confusing these streets can be!" With sound reasoning like that, there was really no arguing with the plan, or the comment about the streets, for that matter. "I won't be long," she said, then added, "lock the door, and if I'm not back within the hour … HIDE!"

So after rebundling herself, Maggie ventured out once more in the hopes of finding her special friend. It was August 31st now, and all around the summer held on for dear life as a small army of street cleaners prepared for the final night of Augustafest. But in leaving the security of her home for the insecurity of The Fist and Firkin, she was completely oblivious to the set of purple eyes watching her from the bin at the end of the street. For Eleanoir, it seems, had rescued the discarded bowler hat and was now twirling it around menacingly in her hands. "So that's where you live," she said, grinning with bad intent as she walked toward the tiny house 'neath a crowd of ravens all circling above. "Well, I hope she won't mind me dropping by unannounced."

∽

It was Deryn who noticed her first, peering in the window, making him buck and bleat with the utmost terror. Claira saw her next and screamed, not realizing who it was at first. (Though she probably would've screamed anyhow.) "Go away!" Claira shouted at her through the glass.

"Please," implored Eleanoir. "I've come to apologize! If you'd only hear me out, I promise everything will be different," she said and then wept unexpectedly. (And though the thought did cross Claira's mind that this could all very well be just an act, she had to admit, it sure looked convincing!) Claira glanced over at Lucky to get his trusted opinion, which mostly involved vigorously shaking his head and recoiling in horror. "But she seems so sincere," remarked Claira before drawing a heavy sigh. For her next decision would fly straight in the face of her better judgment. "I'd just like to hear what she has to say … all right?"

And although Lucky was not the least bit "all right" with it, Claira's mind had already been made up. "Wait here," she instructed. "I'm just going to have a quick word with her," she said with a look of guilt and self-doubt that betrayed her valiant attempt at a comforting smile, as she began unlatching the door before heading out into the street.

Deryn watched from the window, unable to hear a word they were saying. And with Claira's back to him, he wasn't able to get a read on her expressions either. All he could see was the face of Eleanoir as she pounded Claira's eardrums with what could only be lies. But Claira Hinterlund's nature was so forgiving and so pure of heart that the very idea that Eleanoir could be anything other than a rather cold and stern stepmother had not even entered her mind. And certainly the notion of her being a witch was something she would not have entertained even in her wildest dreams. For whatever reason, her father had fallen in love with this woman, and maybe (just maybe) it was she and not Eleanoir who was the unreasonable one. Through it all, Deryn's mind screamed, "Don't listen to her!" but to no avail.

About this time, Magnus Hinterlund himself appeared in the street outside Maggie's home as all three formed a tear-filled group hug.

And after what looked like a round of heartfelt apologies, they hugged and cried some more, adding greatly to Deryn's mounting disbelief. The next thing he noticed was Mr. Hinterlund pointing to the bowler hat, which Eleanoir had concealed behind her back. She presented it to him as though hand-picked from the finest boutique.

Claira smiled as her father tried it on, neither one realizing it was most recently worn by a garbage can! All the while, Eleanoir shot knowing glances at Deryn, who she could see in the window, and smiled cruelly at him whenever possible. *Has the world gone mad?* he wondered frantically. And as if to confirm these suspicions, Claira came rushing in and announced in a voice that was much too cheerful for Deryn's liking, "C'mon, Lucky, we're going home!"

This unforeseen development only made him recoil more, to the furthest reaches of the room, which was not all that far if we're being honest. "Lucky, it's going to be fine, trust me," said Claira with eyes still wet from crying. "We've worked it all out! You won't have to stay in the barn anymore, AND Father is going to get Tressa back! It'll be just like old times ... I promise!"

Although Deryn did trust Claira, he knew from experience that this was all just another heartless joke. At the same time, he also knew his mother would be home very soon and thought it best to get Eleanoir as far away from there as possible!

"I just need to write Mrs. Hedlight a quick note to tell her we've gone home," said Claira, who went right to work jotting down the following words:

> Dear Mrs. Hedlight,
> Thank you so much for your generosity. Lucky and I can't possibly thank you enough! As you know, my father is getting married tomorrow, and being his only daughter I felt it was only right that I be there to support him on his big day. I look forward to seeing you (and Mr. Grimsby) soon.
> Love,
> Claira (and Lucky) XO

Soon the fragile family was trotting back to Hinterlund farm with muted optimism on Claira's part, relief on her father's, and slowly simmering vengeance on Eleanoir's. Even so, the sun managed to peek out from behind the clouds to brighten the road before them, for what it's worth.

Well, that's a good sign at least! thought Claira as she struggled to think positively. She wasn't at all sure she could trust Eleanoir, but for her father's sake, she was willing to give her a second chance.

Deryn, though, felt every bit as wounded in the back of that wagon as on the first day he arrived. Claira smiled back at him periodically in the hopes of reassuring her friend, though her attempts were woefully unsuccessful. For his deer senses were telling him that this was all very bad indeed as they drew closer to home like a moth to a flame.

⌒

Meanwhile, back in Hinthoven, Maggie returned to find Claira's note. She had been to The Fist and Firkin, only to come up empty there. The bartender and chambermaid informed her that Crad's room had not been occupied the previous night and were both of the opinion that he must've headed back to Hixenbaugh. This, of course, made absolutely no sense to her. The twins had not seen him, either, which was even more unusual. But as with Deryn, they offered their help to look for him. Understandably, Maggie was quite perplexed by it all. It seemed like everyone she'd ever cared about was either dead or missing. *P'raps I'm the one who's cursed!* she thought as she paused to check her reflection in the mirror. *Oh, the ravages of time.* She sighed and fumbled with her hands. In the next moment her attention was drawn to the same imposing shadow that had caught Deryn's attention not so long ago. Maggie raced to the window just in time to see Tourtière passing by.

But as if somehow sensing that eyes were upon him, he stopped suddenly and turned toward the house as Maggie ducked down to avoid detection. The next time she looked, though, his face was pressed up against the glass and hideously scowling at her!

Rightly startled, Maggie tumbled backward over Deryn's old seat as Tourtière erupted in a volcano of knee-slapping laughter. A moment later, however, she had rallied all her strength and was back on her feet, shaking a defiant fist at him from the good side of the glass. This only served to make him laugh harder as he headed homeward, leaving behind a terrible feeling that lingered long after he was gone from sight. Maggie slid down the wall and wept for a spell until she had composed herself enough for this one brave thought to shine through. "Well, I think we know where to start looking tomorrow."

For Jacques Tourtière, breakfast meant black coffee, ten pieces of buttered toast, and one raw potato. Like Grimsby, he, too, was a creature of habit, though with a much greater emphasis on the creature part. His house, though only slightly bigger than Maggie's, was packed floor to beams with hunting paraphernalia, rusty tools, and an array of hats and boots and pots and pans. In one corner, an angry wood stove crackled and hissed, while directly opposite to that came a noticeable dip in the floor that sloped down to a filthy cot piled high with coats and trash and bottles and bags. A full chamber pot was positioned perilously close to the kitchen table, which upon closer inspection revealed itself to be a door balancing on a barrel. And all of the above items were thoughtlessly strewn about the room on top of an unusually large bear rug. (Though some things were more off the bear than on.) And while we're on the subject of the bear, the look of anguish it wore appeared to have more to do with its final resting place than any bullet could've ever caused.

The only thing that seemed slightly out of place in the whole cheerless room was a faded floral dress that hung from an old vanity

like the ghost of happiness. Whether it once belonged to his mother or to some long-lost lover, there was just no way of knowing....

On this dreary September morn, Tourtière busied himself with the loading of bullets into a new rifle, which Eleanoir had acquired especially for him. Apparently, they had met not long after she first arrived at Hinthoven, and though completely repulsed by the sight of him, she also could sense in him a sort of relentless mean-spirited quality that just might come in handy someday. And that "someday," it seems, had finally arrived!

For although he tried to hide it, Jacques did have a heart after all. The very idea that an attractive woman had, in his mind at least, befriended him filled his normally solitary existence with a vague sense of something he'd buried along with his childhood. Whether it was love or joy he couldn't say — it had been that long. All he knew was that by granting her this one rather large favour, she would be exceedingly grateful. What that meant exactly could be anyone's guess. Had she promised money? Three wishes? Brandy? Well, whatever it was, it would most certainly be to her benefit alone.

But after tossing back one last gulp of brew, Tourtière stepped out into the dawn's blurry light as a trio of small birds serenaded him sweetly from the rooftop. "Get lost," he fumed and whacked the eave hard with his gun, sending them all off in search of a more hospitable perch.

Then, while locking up the front door, he took a brief moment to scowl upward at the sky, as then a-hunting he did go....

Little did he know that just up the road a little ways, Maggie, Griff, and Gruff had poked their heads out of an archway like a three-headed monster and watched him as he went waddling past. His mind, thankfully, was much too occupied with the day's ominous task to notice he was being watched. And so, as he disappeared around the bend, Maggie and her skeleton crew sprang immediately into action. Griff and Gruff got straight to work on the lock, while Maggie acted as lookout on the off chance that someone should happen along. And as if Bad Timing himself had read the above sentence, the unmistakable sound of a door opening across the road created a flurry of frenzied whispering as Maggie instructed the boys to stop whatever they were doing and act natural. Assuming that was even possible....

In the next instant, our brave souls stood whistling, hands in pockets, while attempting to look nonchalant as the mystery neighbours stepped out into the light. Maggie recognized them right away as that rude elderly couple from the day before! "Mornin', neighbours!" she called to them with a smile and a wave, though all it produced was a similar look of disdain as they walked off without even saying a word. "Some people!" Maggie scoffed. But no sooner had they departed then the clicking of Tourtière's door being unlocked could be plainly heard. "You did it!" exclaimed Maggie. (The word *it* being cut short by Griff's quick hand over her mouth as all three entered Chez Tourtière with the appropriate trepidation.)

Were it not such an urgent mission, the stench alone that greeted their nostrils would have sent all three away screaming in horror. For Grimsby's sake, though, they would brave both the odour and the obstacle course of debris to find their missing friend. At first glance, though, it did not seem even remotely possible that he could be there at all. The house had only one room in it, so unless he was buried 'neath a pile of coats, there was really nowhere to hide Grimsby in such a place. So, with hopes rapidly fading, Maggie and the twins had just turned to look elsewhere when Griff suddenly froze and pointed to the rug under the table.

"What is it?" she asked, her eyes darting from the rug, up to Griff's face, over to Gruff, and back at the rug again. Griff raised a finger to his lips and another to his ear. And as she listened, it wasn't long before she, too, could hear curious noises coming from directly below the bear. "Quick," she said. "Everything out of the way!"

Griff and Gruff wasted no time in moving the table and all other obstacles off to one side, until at last they were able to pull back the rug, revealing a secret door in the floor.

All at once the mysterious sounds became more audible. "Well, don't just stand there, boys, open it up!" And in two shakes of a lamb's tail, the twins were down on all fours and pulling open the trap door, which, as suspected, led to a dark cellar. "Mr. Grimsby? Are you down there?" hollered Maggie as a series of muffled words came floating up from the abyss. "Pass me that candle over there, would ya?" she commanded, as Gruff deftly snatched it from the sill, lit it, then handed it to her. And as she climbed down the coarse rope ladder, Maggie aimed the candle in all directions 'til suddenly it illuminated the face, but curiously not the rest of Grimsby. For as she would soon discover, he was rolled up in a filthy carpet on the floor and gagged.

"My heavens, Crad!" she exclaimed.

The spirited noises that followed assured her that he was still very much alive and kicking, to her enormous relief. Maggie rushed to his side and pulled out the gag (which consisted of a small potato held in place by one of Tourtière's awful knee socks).

"Thank goodness!" he croaked as Maggie went straight to work unrolling him from his humiliating cocoon.

"Poor thing," she said and shook her head with dismay. "Are you all right?"

"I'm much better now," he replied (and, in fact, he did seem to be in pretty good spirits, all things considered). "I thought I would die down here!" he admitted as a small tear rolled down his broad cheek.

"You thought wrong!" said Maggie. "You're not getting rid of me that easily!" she vowed with a smile as both laughed gratefully before tightly embracing.

A few minutes later, as he emerged stiff but otherwise happy from Tourtière's cellar of misery, Grimsby thanked the boys profusely while his eyes adjusted to the welcome light.

"If you don't mind," he said, "I'd very much like to leave this horrible place without delay." And who could blame him?

Soon our heroes went rushing back to the relative safety of Maggie's place, who upon arrival lit the stove to heat up some leftover soup and a soothing pot of tea. She had hoped the rest of the day would be somewhat less exciting than the morning, but sadly this was not to be. For the one perk of being a prisoner in that echoey dungeon was that Crad had been able to overhear most of Eleanoir's wicked plans as she relayed them to Tourtière.

"They're going to kill Mr. Hinterlund," he said. "We must warn Claira."

"But I thought they were getting married today?" Maggie wondered aloud with a look of confusion that was aimed at the floor.

"Yes, they are," he replied. "But it's not the wedding I'm worried about!"

Grimsby began to spill over with all the sordid details he'd been privy to while wrapped up in that awful rug as Maggie and the bouncers listened in hushed silence.

After the wedding ceremony, Magnus and Eleanoir were to take a stroll through the woods alone. (Once they'd signed all the papers, of course.) For she had feigned interest in visiting some of his favourite childhood haunts under the ruse of getting to know him better. What Magnus didn't know was that Tourtière would also be in the woods stalking them, until at such and such a time and such and such a place he would end Magnus's life with a single shot, as though it were just a simple hunting accident. His further instructions were to ditch the gun and head for The Willow Tree on the other side of the woods, where he was to lay low, so to speak, until the coast was clear. And after it had all blown over, Eleanoir promised to pay him handsomely for his role in what she saw as the perfect crime. And once Magnus was out the way, she would then figure out what to do with the other troublemakers.

Well, if it wasn't for all the jaws dropping on the floor you would've heard a pin drop. For Maggie, who was never at a loss for words, was quite frankly at a loss for words. And Griff and Gruff, who were men of few words, were left with even fewer words than usual. This sort of evil was just too confusing for kind-hearted people like Maggie Hedlight to comprehend, and so all she could do was shake her head and mourn for the entire human race. (There was more to the story that Crad chose not to tell, concerning the deer, or more specifically, WHO the deer was. Though he wasn't sure if she'd believe him, anyway.)

"So what do we do now?" asked Maggie, who after her first taste of heroism that morning felt she was ready to go back for seconds.

"One thing's for certain," said Grimsby, looking all three squarely in the eyes. "We need to get out there and warn them … if it's not already too late!"

"But how are we to get out there in time?" asked Maggie. "I can't run as fast as I used to." (And judging by Grimsby's appearance, one could safely assume that he hadn't done much running lately either!)

But before he had a chance to respond to the question of their physical realities, Griff began excitedly tapping the window and pointing to the street as Gruff smiled and nodded enthusiastically beside him.

Maggie and Crad rushed over to the window to see what had grabbed the twins' attention so and were amazed, too, by what they saw. For just then, a florist's delivery carriage had pulled up right out front! And as they watched from the window, a thin man in a tidy uniform was seen carrying a few choice bouquets into a nearby dress shop. Though it wasn't so much the man but the unattended carriage they were interested in! "It's now or never," said Grimsby and then, rather heroically, "destiny calls!"

Without a moment to spare, our courageous four climbed aboard and were away in seconds, leaving the confused florist in the dust of some higher purpose. (Though carriage theft was something they would most certainly have to answer for later on!)

"Have you ever driven one of these things before?" asked Maggie with understandable concern. For it looked as though Crad could be yanked out of his seat at any given moment!

"Well, it has been a while," he hollered back over the screams of pedestrians diving for cover. Maggie closed her eyes and folded her hands in prayer as the carriage sped through town, spilling flowers, knocking over fruit stands, and lastly ripping through a large Augustafest banner as they neared the old Hinthoven sign at the crossroads of town. From here on in, there would be nothing but wide-open country road to Hinterlund Farm. Crad looked over at Maggie, whose eyes remained shut tight, though her hands had gone from prayer position to something resembling eagle talons as she held on for dear life.

"You can open your eyes now," he said, playfully jabbing her arm. Maggie opened one eye at a time before peeking over at Grimsby, now fully laughing at her.

"How can you laugh at a time like this?" she scolded (while trying not to laugh herself). "Especially after all you've been through!" she added before laying her head affectionately on his shoulder. Crad's heart had become emboldened just from having met this remarkable woman. A woman who'd not only saved his life but had also made him a better man. Why, he hardly recognized himself anymore! Who was this stranger in the stolen carriage, off to rescue the fair maiden? Certainly not Cradleigh Thorold Grimsby! For that man lived in fear, and this man wasn't afraid anymore.

"Well, whoever it is," he smiled inwardly, "he could not have come at a better time."

And watching him throughout his moment of soul-searching, Maggie was feeling quite grateful herself. *It's really quite a handsome face*, she thought. *Most importantly, it's a kind face.*

With all the craziness of the past few days, he had yet to tell her all the things he had meant to say before he was so rudely abducted. She was not the least bit concerned, however. "There'll be plenty of time for talking. All the time in the world." And as they returned to the serious mission at hand, their eyes met briefly in the understanding of something that words could not adequately express. "That was some special steering you did back there," she said, shaking her head and chuckling at the memory as they raced t'ward Hinterlund farm now looming in the distance.

"Oh, that wasn't me," replied Crad with a sly wink. "I don't know who it was, but I can assure you it wasn't me."

CHAPTER 19

ENOUGH AS IT IS
(IN SIX PARTS)

Little Grimsbys and Blackberry Pie

ust a cherubic boy of twelve he was the day the witch came calling. And with Merthaloy little more than a toddler, he was oft times expected to babysit while their mother ran errands. Not that he minded very much, for Merthaloy was never any trouble, and besides, he truly loved her with all his heart. But on this drizzly autumn day with our two young Grimsbys home alone, there came a curious rap at the front door. They were not expecting any company, so it was with great interest that Crad went to investigate and found on their doorstep a rather odd-looking woman carrying an unusually large pie.

"Hello, young man, is your mother in?" asked the mysterious lady.

"She's out at present," said Crad as Mertha peeked 'round his leg.

"Oh, I see," replied the woman, pursing her lips. "Well, no matter, I've been asked to leave this pie with the man of the house."

"You have?" asked Crad. "By who?"

"Why, your mother, of course, silly," she said, wiggling her fingers at Merthaloy, now crouching behind Crad and peeking through his legs, as she held the pie out to him. "What a peculiar boy!"

"I don't understand," said Crad, looking first at the pastry and then back at the bearer of it. "What would she do that for?"

"Because she loves you, of course! Mmm ... blackberry pie baked fresh this morning." Her soothing voice spoke as she floated her hand delicately around the circumference of the tempting pastry.

"But we don't have any money for pie," said Crad, who could not have been more mystified if a polar bear had offered him free tickets to the carnival.

"Well, it's your lucky day, then," came her purple-eyed response. "Because *this* pie is free!"

Fortunately for Crad, he had the good sense to know when something didn't feel quite right. He took the pie from her anyway, mostly to be rid of her, and though their mother had always warned them never to accept candy (or in this case pie) from a stranger, he felt she would understand. Crad set it down on the counter and watched from the window as she backed away from the house, all the while making fork-to-mouth gestures in an overtly seductive manner.

And as she crossed the street, he also noticed a curious girl somewhere between his own age and that of his sister apparently waiting for this woman (who he assumed was her mother), along with a large dog that whimpered frantically and strained hard at his leash. Before turning to leave, the young girl looked back at Crad (who she could see in the window) and smiled at him with bright eyes that would linger in his memory from that day forward.

A few hours later, after their mother had returned home, she listened with enormous pride to her son's handling of the curious pie incident. For she had certainly not ordered one. She was mostly relieved to know they had not eaten any of it. But after the kids were asleep in their bed (and I do mean bed singular), their mother (whose name, incidentally, was Marionetta) passed the time as usual, drowning her sorrows and generally feeling sorry for herself. It had not been very long since her man had up and left them all in search of a more carefree existence, or at least that's what she assumed....

Then, looking down at the pie through a haze of aromatic pipe smoke, she found herself marvelling at the intricate pastry work, not to mention the tempting berry filling that bubbled up through a hole in the centre. All at once she felt powerless to resist its golden, flaky charms. *Surely one piece couldn't hurt*, she thought and reached for a blunt knife in the drawer. Well, by the next morning that pie had been completely devoured as Marionetta woke to the worst tummy ache she had ever had. From then on, it seemed, her health went from bad to worse, until less than a year later she was dead from unknown causes, turning two relatively happy children into two sad orphans.

And coincidentally or not, it was a blackberry pie that Tressa Mundy held with oven mitts as the stolen carriage came speeding up the drive (just narrowly missing the minister, who was at that moment heading back into town). For Tressa, it seems, had returned to Hinterlund Farm at the behest of Magnus on his big day. She always believed in taking the high road whenever possible. Even when it meant breaking her own heart!

"Claira?" Tressa's charming voice rang throughout the house. "Were you expecting Mrs. Hedlight?"

The graceful piano music that wafted in from the next room ended abruptly as Claira rushed to the window, just in time to see Mr. Grimsby helping Mrs. Hedlight down from the carriage. (Though Griff and Gruff thought it best to hang back with the few remaining bouquets.)

"Well, that's odd," said Claira. "We weren't expecting them today. Do we have enough food?"

"By the looks of it," Tressa replied skeptically as she set the pie down to cool, "I don't think they've come to eat." In the next instant, Crad and Maggie appeared in the doorway, both slightly out of breath from their short jog.

"Mr. Grimsby, Mrs. Hedlight, what a surprise!" said Claira. "I believe you know Tressa Mundy?" To which Maggie smiled uncertainly. Grimsby, though, seemed much more interested in the pie.

"That's not blackberry, is it?" he inquired.

"Yes, it is," replied Tressa curiously. "It's Miss Eleanoir's favourite."

Grimsby bristled and placed both hands on his head. "Why, it's even worse than I thought!" he said as, to the shock of all those in attendance, he snatched up the pie, ran it outside, and threw it hard against an unsuspecting tree. Grimsby re-entered the house, wiping both hands and looking greatly relieved by his bizarre actions.

"What's the meaning of this!" Claira demanded.

"Listen carefully, dear," said Maggie as all gathered 'round in a show of support. "We believe your father might be in danger. Do you know where he is now?"

"He's in the woods, with Eleanoir," replied Claira with a puzzled look. "They were just married this morning. I-I don't understand, why would he be in danger?" she asked. "Is it Eleanoir?" (To which Deryn bobbed his head up and down excitedly.)

"We can explain later," said Crad. (The deer's reaction was not lost on him.) "So, do you have any idea where in the woods exactly?" he added.

"I think so," said Claira, for she'd just been going over it in her mind. "There's a place my father always loved as a boy. He's taken me there on many occasions."

"Can you take us there now?" Maggie asked while placing both hands on Claira's delicate shoulders. "Time is of the essence, dear."

"Why, yes, yes, of course," said Claira as if waking from a bad dream. "Come quick, I'll show you!" And with that she climbed up on her faithful deer and was off in seconds, with our ragtag crew following close behind.

Meanwhile, Back in the Woods

agnus and Eleanoir lingered awhile by a tree near a pond where as a boy he would swing from a rope into the cool water on hot summer days. (A new rope was hanging there, presumably for the same purpose.) "It was such a lovely wedding," said Eleanoir. "I'm glad we didn't have a big ceremony, aren't you?"

"Yes," said Magnus, still wearing the bowler hat she'd given him. "You know Camilla and I, we had quite a big wedding and ..."

Eleanoir held a finger to his lips, effectively hushing him in mid-sentence. "This is our wedding day. Are we really going to talk about her on our wedding day?"

"You're right," Magnus replied sheepishly. "I'm sorry, I never should've mentioned it."

"It's all right, Mags," she said as she kissed him sweetly 'neath the old swinging tree. "Just don't let it happen again!" Now, aside from it being a very passionate kiss indeed, it was also the cue to let Tourtière know that for Magnus Hinterland, time had run out.

For as planned, Tourtière had been stalking them all morning and now had a clear and easy shot. And so, crouching down behind a small row of bushes, he squinted his coal-black eyes and aimed for the back of Magnus's head. "He won't even know what hit him," he snickered while greedily caressing the gun with his trigger finger. But just as he was set to open fire, Tourtière himself was struck in the back of the head, and by a hoof no less, as Big Eyes came sailing down through the air, yelling, "DEF-A-STATED" all the way. The force of the blow sent Tourtière tumbling off in one direction as the bullet went flying off in another.

"Idiot!" Eleanoir blurted out as Magnus ducked down and then shaded his eyes to where the shot was fired.

"Idiot?" he repeated. For he could plainly see a commotion coming from yonder bushes. "Eleanoir?" he asked curiously. "Who were you talking to? Who's up there?"

Eleanoir cursed under her breath but said nothing more as she began meditating on a brand new spell.

Sadly and Unbeknownst

But sadly, and unbeknownst to the newlyweds, the stray bullet had ricocheted off the swinging tree and straight into Lucky's human heart. For he was at that moment racing toward them with Claira on top as Grimsby and the boys picked up the rear. And waiting back at the Hinthoven sign, Maggie and Tressa had heard the shot, as well, filling their hearts with much dread, and for good reason. For as the bullet hit Lucky, Claira was thrown like a rag doll to the ground, rendering her completely unconscious. And although Grimsby tried his best to revive her, sadly, there was no response. Looking to his left, he could tell at a glance that it was already too late as far as Lucky was concerned. For the time being, at least, Claira would be spared what would surely be a devastating loss for her whenever she came to. Or if she ever came to … So after instructing the twins to stay back with Claira, Grimsby marched boldly into the fray. "This is just awful," he said through a veil of stinging tears. "What have I gotten myself into!" as he disappeared clumsily through the trees.

Too Late

As for Big Eyes, he'd not stopped kicking Tourtière since we last saw them. But now his senses were telling him that a very bad thing had just occurred. So with this in mind, he decided to let The Round One go free as he galloped off in search of his deer friend, not yet knowing that it was, sadly, too late.

Eleanoir and Magnus

Eleanoir, though, had neither moved a muscle nor had she uttered a single word since we last saw her. For she was all consumed with conjuring up the perfect spell for an oblivious husband who was still demanding answers. "Eleanoir? I'm talking to you!" he said firmly. "Who's up there? Is it Tourtière?" As usual, it was all she could do to keep from laughing at the absurdity of the situation she found herself in. "I should've listened to Claira," he said and threw his hands up in frustration. "You know, she warned me about you!"

"Did she really? Well, maybe you should have," replied Eleanoir and cackled cruelly, pushing Magnus to his wit's end.

"Eleanoir! Look at me when I'm talking to you!" he shouted and spun her around by the arm, which succeeded at least in getting her attention. The glaring eyes that betrayed her smile could no longer conceal the hatred she felt for him and his kind. "Who are you?" he uttered, though under his breath, all the while backing up toward the pond. "*What* are you?"

"Oh, I'm going to enjoy this!" she sneered, all the while floating her thin fingers to the sky and nodding her head slowly.

But as fate and perhaps good timing would have it, Grimsby came crashing through the forest, looking every bit a sweaty, hyperventilating mess, while yelling, "Stop right there!" at the top of his lungs.

Eleanoir glanced over her shoulder at the source of this interruption with eyes full of pity. "Mr. Grimsby!" her voice practically sang. "How nice of you to show up!" Magnus, for his part, could only look on in confusion at the arrival of this complete and total stranger. "You've escaped, I see!" she continued and clapped her hands slowly. "Bravo! Last time I saw you, you were snug as a bug in a rug!" she said and smiled at the memory. "No hard feelings, I hope?" After which her full attention was brought back to her clueless husband. "Now, where was I?" she wondered aloud as Magnus's mind raced feverishly.

And as it did so, Crad's mind went racing, too! From his mother and the pie to his sister's disappearance. From there it raced onward to the plight of the Hedlights before finally arriving at his own ordeal in Tourtière's cellar. This cauldron of evil, slowly simmering for years, had now reached its boiling point. His brain was a whistling kettle, his body an angry bull. And all the while the pond was beckoning to him: "Witches and water DO NOT MIX. Witches and water DO NOT MIX." For the first time in his life, he felt the rush of violence coursing through his veins as he kicked up the dirt beneath his feet and charged at Eleanoir with every flab of his being. She had not even a second to react as Grimsby came at her, screaming all the way.

And upon Crad tackling her at full speed, Magnus himself was helpless to do anything but be tackled along with them as all three fell with an enormous splash into the cold water.

Aftermath

It is said that her screams of agony could be heard all over Hinthoven and Hixenbaugh. Even as far as Hannelore!

But when they had finally subsided, there was really nothing left of Eleanoir save for some bubbles and purple smoke. A horrifying experience, to say the least, and one that neither man would soon forget. In the immediate aftermath, Grimsby was seen flailing helplessly and might've even drowned if Magnus hadn't pulled him, puffing and panting, back to dry land. T'was in the midst of this heroism that the bowler hat could also be seen floating away on top of the water, though after a few attempts at snagging it with a pointy stick, Crad gave Mr. Hinterlund's pant leg a good tug and shook his head as the bowler floated off for God knows where....

Then, looking down at the waterlogged Grimsby, Magnus grinned and said, "I'm sorry, I don't believe I've had the pleasure."

"Name's Grimsby," replied the man himself, holding out his hand for some much-needed assistance off the ground. "I'm a good friend of Maggie Hedlight," he went on to say as he rose to his feet again (and with less difficulty than usual!).

"I see," said Magnus, eyeing his equally drenched rescuer with heaps of gratitude and respect. "Well, any friend of the Hedlights is a friend of the Hinterlunds!"

And as our new friends walked back to their separate worlds of uncertainty, Crad thought it prudent to dispatch a silent prayer to whoever might be listening on the other end of the sky. *It's probably too late for Lucky,* his heart admitted. *But please let Claira be all right.* Then, looking up, he spied the benevolent sun peeking through a hole in the clouds and smiled gratefully. "We've all suffered enough as it is," he said to himself as Magnus walked on ahead in silence with eyes that had seen what could never be unseen.

CHAPTER 20

CHANGES

round the same time that Eleanoir screamed her last scream, a miraculous thing did occur. The miracle, first witnessed by Griff and Gruff and then by Big Eyes, was every bit as peaceful as the witch's demise was painful. For in the lifeless body of Lucky the deer, Deryn could feel his soul exiting, but in a much more agreeable way than the original transformation had been. *So this is what dying feels like*, he thought. Only he wasn't dying at all. For the death of Eleanoir, it seems, had somehow broken the spell! And as Big Eyes looked down on his friend with a waterfall of his own tears, Lucky the deer was slowly but surely changing back into Deryn the boy, and right before his eyes! When he finally came to wearing nothing but the green bow the dress shop had given him, the first face he saw was that of Big Eyes as an enormous tear splashed his cheek. "You big hat rack!" said Deryn (not realizing yet that he'd changed in any way).

"I thought there was something funny about you," replied Big Eyes.

Watching Deryn throughout the duration of this glad event, Big Eyes had become transfixed by something small and shiny rolling off his good friend's chest.

"Deryn?" he asked curiously. "What's that over there?" Deryn looked to his right and saw what appeared to be a gold projectile lying in the grass.

"It's a bullet!" he remarked. Then added, "Did that come from me?" and shuddered at the thought.

"I think it came from The Round One," replied Big Eyes matter-of-factly. "Although you might want to hold on to that," he went on and then smiled reassuringly. "I have a feeling he won't be coming back for it."

The next faces Deryn saw belonged to Griff and Gruff, who looked down on either side of Big Eyes like salt and pepper shakers. "Hey, it's … you guys!" said Deryn. "Is my mother here, too?"

"She's not," said Griff, wiping a tear away. "But she's very close!"

"And just wait until she sees you," added Gruff. "It's a miracle!"

"Well, I'd say it was more of a deer-ical," Big Eyes chimed in, though only Deryn could hear him.

"HA! Deer-ical!" He laughed and wondered why nobody else did. It was then that he looked down at his hands and realized he was all human again. Even so, he had somehow managed to retain the ability to com-municate with Big Eyes (and all animals apparently, for just then he could hear a couple of rude birds comparing his body to that of a small white twig).

But looking down the full length of his body, he soon came to realize that he was completely naked and so began covering up those bits of himself he did not wish to share with the rest of the world. Ever the gentleman, Griff pulled off his long sweater and handed it to Deryn. It ended up looking more like a dress on him, truth be told, especially with that green bow around his neck, as he rose to his feet and took stock of all his fingers and toes.

Upon hearing faint moaning sounds in the vicinity, Deryn looked to his left and saw Claira on the ground, seemingly waking from a spell of her own. "Claira!" he gasped and rushed to her side as the rest of the gang looked on, greatly relieved to see her amongst the living again. And as she opened her eyes, the first face SHE saw belonged to Deryn Hedlight, who had somehow gotten more handsome, or so she thought, since last they met!

"Deryn?" She questioned her own eyes while looking around in a panic. "Am I dead?"

"No, Claira, you're alive. We're both alive!" he said, smiling down on her in the bright sunshine.

"But where's Lucky? And why are you wearing his bow? Lucky!" she called out, struggling to sit up as Deryn struggled to calm her down.

"Claira," he said softly. "Look at me … I AM Lucky!" And as she studied his face, it wasn't long at all before she could see that same frightened deer whose life she had spared not so long ago. But most importantly, she recognized her best friend. And when they kissed for the first time, all that was wrong became instantly righted as the twins and even Big Eyes beamed at one another with hearts full and bright.

A few moments later, Grimsby and Mr. Hinterlund were seen coming around the bend, drenched but otherwise well. Crad's worried expression changed instantly to relief upon seeing Claira up and about. (Though he had mistaken Big Eyes for Lucky and wondered who the odd-looking boy was.)

"Deryn Hedlight?" exclaimed Magnus as if seeing a ghost. "Is that really you?" he asked with more energy in his voice than anyone could recall.

"Yes, sir!" he said. "It's really me!"

"But how? And why are you wearing a dress?" a stunned Magnus inquired to the amusement of almost everyone there. It was all Grimsby could do to look around in awe from Deryn to Big Eyes, over to Claira, then back at Mr. Hinterlund (who had not stopped looking at Deryn) as Claira rushed to her father and gazed up into his blue, astonished eyes.

"And Eleanoir?" she asked. To which he could only sigh regretfully.

For it was all Mr. Hinterlund could do to look around in awe at the small gathering before pouring out his normally reserved heart. "I can't tell you how grateful I am … to all of you. For all of you. And how truly sorry I am for allowing myself to be so blind."

Then, seizing the moment for himself, Deryn felt this as good a time as any to pour his own heart out as he cleared his throat to address the modest assembly of friends before him. "I'd like you all to meet Big Eyes," he began. "I wouldn't be here if not for him. He was a friend when I needed one most." Here he paused to look out over the bright faces all smiling back. (Although Big Eyes seemed mostly embarrassed by the attention.)

"And Claira?" Deryn continued. "I may not be able to carry you around like I used to, but Big Eyes certainly can, and if your father would permit him to take Lucky's place in that regard, I'd be forever grateful," he concluded then bowed his head in anticipation of Mr. Hinterlund's response.

But Magnus, who had still not fully grasped where Lucky had gone to, or even how Deryn got there, could only answer, "Well, I guess I don't see why not!" to the eruption of cheers as Claira squeezed him harder than ever before.

Grimsby then winked at Deryn (who as usual winked right back). For they both understood without saying a word that there was somebody they needed to see, and right away.

⌔

For Maggie and Tressa had been on the fence, literally, this whole time. They had heard the gunshot and the screams, of course. But it had been some time since they'd heard anything more, and so naturally they were both beyond concerned.

"I sure hope Claira and her father are okay; Crad, too, of course. He's become very special to me," said Maggie, glancing over at Tressa, whose smile, as always, held just the right amount of kindness.

"I'm sure it was Miss Eleanoir we heard screaming," Tressa said. "I've known Claira her whole life, and that didn't sound like her at all!"

Maggie heaved a sigh of relief and said, "You're probably right," while noticing Tressa's elegant profile for the first time. "You know, you're a very attractive girl," she remarked. "And such a caring person, too."

Tressa didn't quite know where all this was heading, but Maggie elaborated in short order. "Don't you have somebody special in your life, dear? Someone you love?" she asked, not meaning to pry.

Tressa looked down at their four feet dangling and replied, "Yes, I am in love with someone, but it just so happens that someone was married today!"

Maggie's mouth opened in surprise before spreading warmly into a smile that ran the entire width of her face.

"Well, judging by the sound of that scream," offered Maggie, "I don't think it's going to last!" This she said with an ironic wink as they bumped shoulders and giggled like old school chums in a moment of unexpected gallows humour.

It was in the midst of this camaraderie that Tressa noticed our heroes returning. "Look!" she said and pointed excitedly. "They're coming!"

And indeed they were. Maggie strained her eyes toward the oncoming entourage of friends now fast approaching. And although she couldn't quite make them out yet, there was something victorious in the way they walked, or at least it seemed that way. She could see Claira on top of who she assumed was Lucky and the loping mountain range that could only be Griff and Gruff. "Oh, and there's Mr. Grimsby!" she sighed with a hand over her heart. "And Mr. Hinterlund, too!" Maggie nudged Tressa with her elbow. "He's so handsome!"

"Yes, I know!" Tressa replied, her eyes now brimming with grateful tears.

"Well, that's odd," said Maggie, shading her eyes with both hands. "Now, who's that little girl there walking beside Claira?"

"What little girl?" asked Tressa, squinting forward herself. But as their friends drew nearer, the face of the mystery girl became more and more familiar to her.

"I don't think that's a girl," said Tressa, who then let out a soft shriek before adding, "oh, Mrs. Hedlight."

Maggie searched Tressa's eyes curiously for a moment before returning to the girl in question, until suddenly, as though her heart had recognized him first, she lifted both hands to her face and burst into tears. Without wasting one second more, Maggie hopped down from the fence and ran to her boy, crying all the way. Deryn came running, too, until both met halfway in a tear-filled embrace that was more joyful than anything the old Hinthoven sign had ever witnessed before. Naturally, the faces that would soon gather 'round them were all moist with happy tears that rolled from soft cheeks to the green grass below.

And as they walked back to Hinterlund Farm to enjoy the feast Tressa had prepared (but mostly each other's company), Crad walked arm in arm with Maggie and was convinced she could not have looked more beautiful if she tried. "You did this!" he said, gently tapping her wrist. "Because you never gave up on your boy!"

"Well, I did have my doubtful days," she admitted. "But you helped me through them, Crad Grimsby, and now you're stuck with me!" This stolen moment, which they followed up with a tender kiss, was happily noticed by Deryn and Claira.

"I hope we're just like them when we're older." She smiled.

"Older? I for one have no intention of growing old," said Deryn. "You and I will stay young forever, isn't that right, Big Eyes?"

"If that's what your five senses are telling you," came his predictably droll response, to which Deryn laughed, and much too loudly.

"I keep forgetting, I'm the only one who can hear him," he said, before nervously whistling and puffing his cheeks awkwardly.

"Silly boy!" said Claira as they drifted off in a vast dream of happiness.

Trailing behind the pack ever so slightly came Magnus and Tressa. During the emotional reunion at the Hinthoven sign, he had caught a glimpse of her eyes and all the tear-filled kindness they held. It was as though he were seeing her for the first time. *She's absolutely lovely*, a voice inside of him said. And as they walked together, he told her as much. "Tressa, I'm an idiot."

"Sir, you are not," she said, though to his hand now raised in objection.

"No, let me finish. You see, I *am* an idiot, and I'll tell you why. Because I took you for granted, and that was wrong. But mostly it's because you were the best thing that ever happened to Claira and myself, but I sent you away."

Tressa's heart was beating so loudly now, she was convinced it would explode right then and there. "Oh, Mr. Hinterlund," she implored. "I understand, it wasn't you, it was her."

"Yes, it was her," he admitted. "But even so, I never should have fallen for it. I put my whole world in jeopardy, and that was inexcusable! Oh, and please call me Mags," he added with his trademark grin now fully on display.

"But how could you have known?" Tressa began to say when he raised a hand once more to continue.

"The biggest reason, though, that I'm an idiot," he said, "is because … I never noticed how incredibly beautiful you are."

Tressa's eyes overflowed as she looked to the ground and began to tremble.

"And if you let me," he went on while firmly holding on to her shoulders, "I promise to tell you just how beautiful you are with every passing day for as long as we live, and longer if possible." And with that, a kiss took place that was witnessed by all, adding greatly to the abundance of smiles and happy tears, while brightening up all their lives in the process.

For love had truly lifted the world from its place of loss and loneliness, only to replace it with friendship and fulfillment of which was there was seemingly no end. And what with this being a fairy tale and all, as you might have guessed, they all lived happily ever.... Well, you know.

EPILOGUE

In the weeks and months following Eleanoir's death, Hinthoven basked in the glow of many changes. At Hinterlund Farm, for example, a double wedding took place as Magnus married Tressa and Crad married Maggie. A third knot might've also been tied, but then Deryn and Claira were only seventeen, and neither one of them was in any hurry to grow up just yet. Besides, this was Magnus's only daughter, and he hoped, like all fathers, to someday throw a big reception and pull out all the stops, so to speak. The other major development was that Crad, having signed over The Willow Tree to Charlisle, had now acquired The Fist and Firkin! He gave it a fresh coat of paint, added a few new windows to make it less dreary, and changed the letter T to an H, renaming it The Fish and Firkin! Griff and Gruff were kept on to help with the day-to-day operation, as well as providing security when necessary. Though with all the new and colourful changes he'd made, most of the unsavoury customers had stopped coming altogether!

Soon it became less infamous and more famous for serving the best fish 'n' chips in town. (If you're ever in Hinthoven … just saying.)

The florist, too, had forgiven Crad for running off with his carriage (not to mention all the bouquets that were lost or damaged). It didn't hurt that Magnus hired him to supply all the roses for the double wedding! And as well, Deryn and Claira both took on jobs at the flower shop after school. For she'd become quite gifted at floral arrangements, and Deryn and Big Eyes handled all the deliveries. There was just something about having a personal bouquet delivered by a handsome boy riding on a deer that made sales go through the roof! In other news, wanted posters for Jacques Tourtière had been plastered throughout the land for kidnapping and attempted murder. Though no one knew for sure whatever became of him. There were rumours he had choked on a potato and died, while many believed he'd been eaten by a family of bears. At any rate, nobody was all that sad to see him go, and least sad of all was Crad Grimsby. He even spearheaded a movement to have the Tourtière house condemned as a safety hazard, which was unanimously agreed upon by everyone on city council. People were mostly happy that a sense of normalcy had returned to Hinthoven, in all its boring glory.

The Hinterlunds and the Hedlights (along with Mr. Grimsby) became as close as any family could ever be and would get together regularly for holidays and even Sunday roasts. Best of all, Big Eyes no longer had to live in fear of hunters or hide in caves. He had a home now with two of the best friends a deer could ever hope for.

With the death of Eleanoir came many unconfirmed reports of other spells being broken in various townships along the peaceful river. Come to think of it, in a little room just above the Lonely View Tavern, Sallee (now the innkeeper's widow) was busy cleaning Crad's old chamber one afternoon when a middle-aged woman chillingly appeared next to the window. As you can imagine, this gave Sallee such a fright that she ran screaming all the way down the stairs. Merthaloy looked over at the willow tree for a moment before realizing where she was. And then, checking herself in the vanity, she could hardly believe her eyes! Her face, though still childlike, was now set in the body of a much older woman. How much time had she lost?

And where was her big brother? These were the questions foremost on her mind as she descended the staircase as in days of old.

But Sallee, who was now cowering in the kitchen, could barely even look up as Mertha walked over to the sink where she had once washed the dishes and looked out on all the birds and squirrels. "Sallee? It's me, Merthaloy," she said. "Don't you remember?"

This only served to make Sallee tremble more as she covered her ears and cried, "You're not real," while attempting to shut her eyes tighter than was humanly possible.

"Sallee, look at me, I'm as real as you are," Mertha implored and held out her hand. "Here, see for yourself." And so, after gathering all her nerve, Sallee took hold of Merthaloy's lily-white hand, looked in her eyes, and knew right away that it was truly her. A little older, perhaps, but every bit as real as on the day she had disappeared. There was so much to talk about, it seemed, but Merthaloy had lost enough time as it was. All she wanted was to find her brother as soon as possible. The only news Sallee had ever received from Crad, though, was that he worked at an inn called The Willow Tree. But that was over twenty years ago, and she'd heard nothing since.

So it was that early the next morning, Merthaloy set out for The Willow Tree, where she was relieved to find out that not only was her brother still alive, but that he was married and living in Hinthoven, of all places!

Always the gentleman, Charlisle even offered to escort her through the woods himself. An offer, though, that was politely declined. For this was a journey she just had to make on her own! As she neared the edge of the forest on the Hinthoven side, she stopped to take a sip from the same pond, incidentally, where Eleanoir had met her demise. *It's so lovely here*, she thought as all around the shades of night began to fall. She even took a few swings on a rope that childhood had left behind. It was in mid-swing, in fact, when she looked up at the branches and saw there an unkindness of ravens all nesting in a strange bowler hat. "Where'd you get that from?" she giggled. And as she climbed up the ancient tree, the ravens would soon surrender their nest without a fight and fly off for safer branches.

So with the hat firmly in her possession and her feet on solid ground, she began to shake out all that the birds had left behind. In doing so, she couldn't help but notice the strange inscription on the inside. "C.O.W. Hixenbaugh," Mertha read out loud. "Well I'll be …" She had thought to purchase a wedding gift for Crad in town, but this seemed almost predestined. "He's going to love it," she said, placing it proudly on her head. But then how could he not? It was from their hometown, after all!

So at this time we say goodbye to Merthaloy, now off in search of her big brother for what will surely be a joyful reunion, with a raven's nest for a hat and a touch of twilight in her eyes. As to the rhythm of her footsteps on gravel, an old schoolyard song returns to keep her company as the sleepy candlelit town flickers in the distance. Her shadow is practically there!

Leaves in the whirlwind, scarecrow's clappin',
All good children ought to be nappin'.

THE END

The Mariposa Folk Festival
Michael Hill

Mariposa began in the heyday of the early 60s "folk boom." In its more than fifty-five years, it has seen many of the world's greatest performers grace its stages: Pete Seeger, Joni Mitchell, Leonard Cohen, Gordon Lightfoot, Buffy Sainte-Marie, Jann Arden, and Serena Ryder.

The festival has long held a musical mirror to popular culture in Canada. It thrived during the folk boom years and the singer-songwriter era of the early 70s. Its popularity dipped during the rise of disco and punk as the 70s wore into the early 80s. And it nearly died due to lack of interest in the 90s — the age of grunge and new country, and the golden age of CD sales. Thanks to a recent wave of independent, home-grown music, Mariposa is having a resurgence in the early twenty-first century. Audiences have always come and gone, but the festival has stayed true to its mandate: to promote and preserve folk art in Canada through song, story, dance, and craft.

Festival Man
Geoff Berner

Travel in the entertaining company of a man made of equal parts bullshit and inspiration, in what is ultimately a twisted panegyric to the power of strange music to change people from the inside out.

At turns funny and strangely sobering, this "found memoir" is a picaresque tale of inspired, heroic deceit, incompetence, and – just possibly – triumph. Follow the flailing escapades of maverick music manager Campbell Ouiniette at the Calgary Folk Festival, as he leaves a trail of empty liquor bottles, cigarette butts, bruised egos, and obliterated relationships behind him. His top headlining act has abandoned him for the Big Time. In a fit of self-delusion or pure genius (or perhaps a bit of both), Ouiniette devises an intricate scam, a last hurrah in an attempt to redeem himself in the eyes of his girlfriend, the music industry, and the rest of the world. He reveals his path of destruction in his own transparently self-justifying, explosive, profane words, with digressions into the Edmonton hardcore punk rock scene, the Yugoslavian Civil War, and other epicentres of chaos.

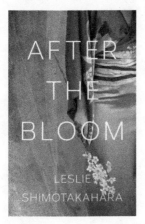

After the Bloom
Leslie Shimotakahara

Lily Takemitsu goes missing from her home in Toronto one luminous summer morning in the mid-1980s. Her daughter, Rita, knows her mother has a history of dissociation and memory problems, which have led her to wander off before. But never has she stayed away so long. Unconvinced the police are taking the case seriously, Rita begins to carry out her own investigation. In the course of searching for her mom, she is forced to confront a labyrinth of secrets surrounding the family's internment at a camp in the California desert during the Second World War, their postwar immigration to Toronto, and the father she has never known.

Epic in scope, intimate in style, *After the Bloom* blurs between the present and the ever-present past, beautifully depicting one family's struggle to face the darker side of its history and find some form of redemption.